OHIO
DOMINICAN
UNIVERSITY™

SINCE 1911

Donated by
Floyd Dickman

Poor Is Just a Starting Place

Poor Is Just a Starting Place

Leslie J. Wyatt

Holiday House / New York

ACKNOWLEDGMENTS

Thanks go to my husband, Dave, for his unfailing love and for always being willing to read the rough drafts. Mention must also be made of my kids, who try not to interrupt my writing time and whose support is unswervingly loyal—thanks, guys.

Special appreciation belongs to my agent, Steven Chudney, editor Regina Griffin at Holiday House, and fellow author Jody Feldman, for their insightful critiques. Last, but not in any way least, thank you to all the people who believed in me and to those who shared their stories about growing up in the Kentucky hills.

Library of Congress Cataloging-in-Publication Data
Wyatt, Leslie J.
Poor is just a starting place / by Leslie J. Wyatt.— 1st. ed.
p. cm.
Summary: During the Great Depression, twelve-year-old Artie Wilson, determined to escape plowing and planting the fields and milking the cow on her family's farm, longs to leave Buck Creek, Kentucky, and her life of poverty.
ISBN 0-8234-1884-7 (hardcover)
1. Depressions—1929—Juvenile fiction. [1. Depressions—1929—Fiction. 2. Family life—Kentucky—Fiction. 3. Poverty—Fiction. 4. Schools—Fiction. 5. Fathers and daughters—Fiction. 6. Kentucky—History—20th century—Fiction.] I. Title.

PZ7.W9682Po 2005
[Fic]—dc22   2004047451

In memory of Granny, who lived
Artie's life and whose determination
was equaled only by her zest for living

Chapter One

"I wouldn't do that if I was you."

Artie Wilson looked up from her history book. The one-room schoolhouse was chilly in the April afternoon, and Miss Small held a corncob soaked in kerosene, which was used for quick-starting a fire in the coal stove each morning.

"What did you say, Ballard?" the young teacher asked.

"I said, I wouldn't do that if I was you—throw that there corncob on top of them smolderin' coals. Kerosene fumes might explode."

Artie watched as her brother unwound his long legs from his too-small desk and stood. "Reckon the stovepipe is all sooted up," he said. "That's why it ain't drawin' like it should. Want I should try and work on it?"

Miss Small closed the stove door and replaced the corncob in the nearby can. "Yes, please, Ballard. Do you need a chimney brush or something?"

Ballard scratched behind his ear. "Well, a brush would be the best. My dad has got one over to home that I can bring on Monday. But right now, I'll just try tappin' on the pipe to knock some of that there soot back down into the stove." He picked up the stove poker and began rapping on the pipe. *Tap. Tap-tap. Tap-tap-tap.* There was a little slithering sound from the stove.

"Is it working?" Miss Small asked.

"Oh, it's a-workin' all right," Ballard said. "Didn't you hear that slippin noise? I'll just keep a-tappin'."

Tap-tap-TAP. TAP-tap. TAP. Artie remembered that when Miss Small had come to replace their old teacher two months ago, she hadn't even known how to start a fire in the stove or trim a lamp wick so it would burn evenly. How strange it would be to grow up in a house with electricity and central heating as Miss Small had. And how far away the big city of Louisville seemed from the tiny burg of Caneyville and this little schoolhouse tucked away in the woods near Buck Creek, deep in the hills of central Kentucky.

TAP-tap. TAP-tap. Ballard stretched high, rapping up the pipe as far as he could reach, then downward to where it joined the stove. A small black cloud seeped from the cracks around the stove door, like the breath of a dragon.

TAP-TAP—There was a scritching, trickling sound, like someone sliding down a gravelly bank. Ballard gave another hearty tap just as Miss Small bent over and opened the door to peer into the stove.

They couldn't have timed it better. A chunk of loosened soot fell out of the pipe onto the smoldering coals in the stove. Thick black smoke belched out of the door, enveloping the teacher and flowing over the students closest to the center of the room.

"EEEeee, eeeEEE, eeeEEE!" Sarah Jane Bratcher set up a steady screeching, reminding Artie of the pig up at Grandpa's place. The rest of the twenty-odd students sat like fence posts.

Miss Small jerked upright. Greasy black dust blanketed her light calico dress, and her eyes stood out like two white eggs in the sudden blackness of her face. Ballard froze, openmouthed, helpless, poker still in hand. Soot continued to spew out the door and onto the teacher, the students, and the already dingy schoolroom.

Artie choked, trying not to laugh at the look on her brother's face as he finally came to life. Dropping the poker, he slammed the stove door shut, then ran to throw open the schoolhouse door. The crisp April air rushed in, fresh with the scent of budding trees and wet Kentucky soil.

As Artie looked at her classmates, now covered in black film, she smothered a giggle. Her seatmate, Eula Jenkins, laughed out loud. Miss Small managed a weak smile, teeth bright in her black face. Soon the whole classroom was whooping with laughter—except Sarah Jane. She snorted while dabbing at the coal dust that had turned her pink ruffled dress to a dirty gray.

"You just make it worse if you rub it in, Sarah Jane," Artie said.

"Mind your own business, Artie Wilson," Sarah Jane said. "You're used to being filthy. *I* am not."

Heat burned up Artie's neck. Stuck-up Sarah Jane—she had a different dress to wear every day, while Artie and most of the other students had only two sets of clothes to their names. She bit back the poison words that threatened to pour out and stalked over to the water bucket that hung by the door, passing Ballard as he ambled back to his seat.

"So, Ballard," Miss Small said, her voice a little strained. "Maybe tapping on the stovepipe wasn't such a good idea?"

"Well." Ballard paused, trying to control his grin. "More'n likely, openin' up the stove door whilst I was tappin' wasn't such a good idea."

Miss Small had the grace to smile. "So I see. I guess this is one lesson none of us will forget." She looked around the schoolroom. Dingy before, now every flat surface wore a film of black and oily soot. The teacher sighed.

Artie stared out the open door at the greening world. Kentucky was waking from winter. New leaves like bright green lace softened black tree branches in the woods just outside. Spring grass blanketed the world in emerald velvet. The afternoon sky reminded Artie of the bright blue flowers that would soon spring up all over the floor of the woods, their tiny five-petaled blossoms like drips of earthbound sky.

Miss Small's voice jerked Artie back to reality. "Artie, please bring that water bucket here so we can wash our faces."

Artie lifted the pail from its hook. "There's just a little bit in here. And it's covered with coal dust. Do you want I should go on down to Doc Miller's place and fetch us some more drinkin'—I mean, drink*ing* water?"

Normally she hated this chore. By the time she had carried a bucket of water from the nearest well, nearly three-quarters of a mile away, her arms felt as if they would fall off, and her dress and shoes would be drenched. But today fetching water would be a chance to escape cleanup duty and to be outside in the springtime world.

Miss Small peered in the tin bucket, then looked out the door. Artie caught a fleeting look of longing pass over her teacher's face. Did she also want to leave the school behind and be part of green-up time?

"Yes, Artie. You may get some more. But don't take all afternoon." Miss Small's voice and manner were firm, yet Artie swore she caught a twinkle of understanding in her eyes.

Artie leaped out the doorway and flung the remaining water over the packed dirt of the tiny schoolyard. Before starting for the well, she set the bucket down and picked her way through the trees on the east side of the school. There was no outhouse at Buck Creek. The boys used the woods on the north side, the girls kept to the east. There was no toilet paper, either. The students relied on grass or any leaves that might be handy. And they watched where they walked.

Artie kept her eyes to the ground as she looked for a likely spot and hurried to finish before any other students came out, then picked her way back to the clearing and the tin bucket. Now she wished she'd saved the last of the water to wash her hands, even if it had been full of coal dust.

Next time I'll think about that, Artie thought as

she gave a skip-hop down the path, swinging the bucket in a circle over her head. Dad was always after her for "going off half-cocked"—acting first, thinking later. Well, maybe he's right, she thought. But at least I *do* things. So many people were born, lived, and died within a few miles of the same place. They just went through each day same as the last and didn't seem to ever *do* anything different.

Artie looked up at the sky that stretched wide and blue above her—stretched far beyond Buck Creek, Caneyville, and the world she knew, reaching to Louisville and to all the places she longed to see.

She swiped the bucket at the brown weeds beside the trail and shouted to the waiting woods, "I'll be saying good-bye to you someday!"

The teacher before Miss Small, Miss Meyers, had grown up about five miles from Caneyville in a family much like Artie's own. But she had gotten away from Caneyville and worked her way through teacher's college.

Artie had turned twelve years old last January. A few more years, and she would hop that train she heard whistling in the distance. Go to Louisville like

Miss Meyers had. Go where the buildings were tall and gracious. Go where the roads never turned to mud and where ladies wore pretty dresses every day.

But for now, maybe she'd disappear in the woods on this April afternoon and not even go back for the last hour of school.

Yet even as she played with the idea, Artie knew she wouldn't do it. She was already behind in school because she'd had to stay home and help out. If she wanted to be a teacher, she'd need to finish school. Besides, the thought of the disappointment on Mom's thin face was like a chain on her ankle, holding her to the path of duty.

Then there was Dad. Though he didn't think much of school, he might get mad anyway.

Dad. A sudden tightness twisted in her chest. He didn't think much of school and he didn't think much of people who went off to the big city and left their home folks. Not that he stayed home much himself, but he sure wasn't keen on anybody else leaving.

She could hear him now. "Now, sister. You can't go off and leave your mom right now. You're the best little helper this side of the Ohio River, and she needs you, what with her TB and all."

The "all" would be the new baby coming in May, of course. *Bang!* Artie whanged the innocent bucket against a nearby tree and then gave a nervous frown as she saw the big dent she'd put in the already tired-looking container.

When she'd tried to talk to her dad before about becoming a teacher, he'd grinned and made a joke of the whole thing. She couldn't help herself—she smiled back. Even now she smiled as she pictured the twinkle in Dad's blue eyes and the deep dimples in his cheek as he'd said, "Now, Artie-gal. Why would a smart girl like you need any more schoolin'? You're already quicker at figures than a frog snappin' flies."

Caught up in her thoughts, Artie came to Doc Miller's little unpainted frame house where the well squatted in the weedy yard. She took a bucket from the well's wooden ledge and dropped it into the dark hole, grasping the rope in one hand. *Splat.* After waiting a few seconds for the pail to sink and fill, she drew it up hand over hand until she could heft it over the edge and pour an inch or two into the school bucket.

After rinsing it clean, she scrubbed the greasy coal dust off her face and skinny arms as best she could, then rinsed the bucket again and poured it full. The water reflected the sky, as if she had scooped up a bucketful of blue.

Artie smiled at the thought, and her teeth showed white on the water-mirror. Ever since Miss Meyers had told her to brush them every day, Artie had faithfully done so. But at the reflection of her faded red dress, she frowned. Every day since school started last fall she'd worn it. Every weekend she washed and ironed it, and the constant wear and washing had faded its bright red to a color halfway between raspberry and tired pink.

Before she'd left for a new position in St. Louis, Missouri, Miss Meyers had said, "Class, I want you to remember—everyone starts somewhere. It's where you go from there that matters. You can be whatever you want to be."

These words had gone down, down, down and lodged in Artie's heart. Even with the Depression sinking its cruel teeth into the nation and with hunger haunting her stomach, she felt a strange lifting each time she thought of those words. She, Artie Wilson, would be a teacher too someday. The thought matched the brightness of the spring afternoon, and she forgot about her faded dress, mouse brown hair, and worn-out shoes.

On the return trip to the schoolhouse, she took it slow and easy, setting the bucket down every so often, stretching out her short freedom. The *cheer-cheer-cheer* of redbirds dominated the woods. Miss Small called them cardinals, but Artie preferred the name redbird. A cardinal could be anything from a label on a baking powder tin to a baseball player, but a redbird could only be a red bird. Their swoop, swoop, swooping flight pattern, like Grandma's shuttle flying back and forth on her loom, wove threads of bright red and reddish yellow through the green lace of the budding trees and bright blue fabric of the sky.

The schoolroom seemed dirtier and stuffier than ever in contrast to the green freshness of the wakening woods. The pervading odor of coal soot now mixed with the usual smells of mouse droppings, damp wool, old sweat, and greasy hair. But the desktops had been wiped off and the floor swept while Artie had been gone, and all the students were back in their seats.

Miss Small reached for the bucket of water. "Thank you, Artie."

Miss Small had an air of culture about her that Artie wanted to acquire. Miss Meyers had been that way too, and she'd taught Artie far more than just how to read and write. Perhaps Miss Small would help her as Miss Meyers had.

While the other children washed their faces, Artie flopped into her seat. Her seat, but not for long, she reminded herself each time she sat down. She would soon finish the fifth-level reader. In fact, she would have been at the sixth level already if she hadn't missed so many school days doing work at home. When she finished the reader—maybe next month—she would move up a grade. And back one desk, to sit with Miss Sarah Jane Bratcher.

Artie wondered how Sarah Jane would react to having someone share her desk. Sarah Jane always presided over the whole double desk, piled her books in the bench beside her, arranged her papers in neat stacks on the desktop to her left, and generally acted like she owned that corner of the world.

"When I move up, I'll give Sarah Jane a run for her money," Artie muttered under her breath.

"What did you say, Artie?" Eula asked.

"Nothing."

"Teacher said there's an essay contest," Eula whispered. "She's goin' to tell us about it, now you're back."

As if she had overheard Eula's words, Miss Small stood and rapped on her battered oak desk to get everyone's attention.

"Now, class," she said. "Today is Friday, April eleventh. As you all know, there will be a graduation ceremony for the class of 1930 on the first Friday in June. Two of our students—Marcus Dockery and Ballard Wilson—will be finishing the eighth grade."

Eighth grade was as far as most students went in school, at least in the rural areas of Kentucky. There was a high school in Caneyville, two and a half miles away from the Wilson's home. Most families didn't have extra money for clothes and supplies to send a student and Artie's family was no exception. But that suited Ballard just fine.

Miss Small continued. "The state teachers school of Kentucky is giving a twenty-five-dollar savings bond to the winner of their upcoming essay contest. All the schools in the area will be competing. The essay will be on the subject of the writer's heritage. Judges will be looking for some interesting stories about your ancestors, why they are unique, and how you feel this has helped make you the person that you are today."

Twenty-five dollars? Artie blinked. That was more cash money than she'd ever seen at one time. It would buy an awful lot of food.

A hand waved. "What's a savings bond, Miss Small?"

"It is like money," Miss Small answered. "But in this case, the teacher's school has said that the winner can only use it for going to high school."

Twenty-five dollars would pay for almost a whole year of high school in Caneyville. Artie grinned. Since it could be used for nothing else, she wouldn't even have to feel guilty about using it for school instead of food, and Dad wouldn't be able to talk her into letting him spend it. All she had to do was write a winning essay, and the money would be hers.

Louisville, here I come, she thought. Closing her eyes, she tried to think of something outstanding about her heritage. Maybe she could tell how, as a little girl, one of her great-grandmothers had come with her family down the Ohio River on a flatboat and settled the uncharted land of Kentucky. Or how her great-great-grandfather had fought in the Civil War. Or what about her third-great-grandfather, the one who had been neighbor to Abraham Lincoln's father over by Hodgenville? She sat up straighter in her seat and pulled out a piece of paper.

Eula waved her hand. "Teacher, I don't understand what you mean."

"Well, Eula," Miss Small said, "is there an important happening in your family that has had a good effect on you?"

A little hand waved from the front row. "Yes, Richard?" It was Eula's seven-year-old brother.

Richard stood, his round, coal-smudged face shiny with pride of knowing. "I know somethin' important and interestin'. My pappy, he done sold a mule at the stock market in Leitchfield jist last week. Traded her off for a hunnerd dollars, and that were right good money, too."

Sarah Jane's silver laughter tinkled in the quiet room. Eula flushed dark red and her grubby fingers tightened into fists. Miss Small frowned and shook her head slightly at Sarah Jane, whose giggles subsided.

The teacher smiled at Richard. "Thank you, Richard. That *is* interesting and important. I'm glad your father made such a good trade. Must have been a pretty mule."

Richard sat down. "Yessum. She were a right pretty mule. Sorta dark with light points, like one o' them big Missouri mules."

Miss Small nodded, then asked, "Can anyone else give an example of how his heritage has helped shape his or her life?"

Artie felt the air stir behind her. Swiveling around

in her seat, she saw Sarah Jane waving a pudgy hand. She might have known Sarah Jane would compete for the savings bond, whether she needed it or not.

"Yes, Sarah?"

Sarah Jane stood up. "My family comes from the Bratchers of Georgia." She said *JOE-ja* for Georgia.

Artie rolled her eyes.

"My great-grandfather was a captain in the army of the Confederacy. We owned a lot of slaves and had a *lot* of land. That's how we came to have such a nice, big house here." Sarah Jane sat back down with a bounce of her long, dark curls.

Artie clenched her teeth.

"Thank you, Sarah," Miss Small said. "Class, I am sure that as you begin to think it over, you will see ways that your heritage has affected your life today.

"The assignment will have to be handed in by the last week of May in order to be judged. I will announce the results on June second, during the last week of school." Miss Small wrote the due date on the blackboard. "Now, please gather your things. You are dismissed for the day. Have a good weekend."

Artie crammed her books into her side of the desk and turned to go. Behind her, Sarah Jane stood up too. They stepped into the aisle at exactly the same moment. Artie was heading for the door at the back of the room, but Sarah Jane was apparently going to the front of the room.

"Excuse me, Artie. I have something to give Miss Small." The words were innocent, but the tone of voice and the curl of the Bratcher lip were anything but angelic.

"Excuse *me,* Sarah Jane. I am goin' the other way." Artie hoped her eyes had taken on the icy blue color that frosted her father's eyes when he was mad. She made her thin legs as solid as two posts.

Sarah Jane tried to push by, but Artie leaned forward and didn't give an inch. Sarah Jane's bottom lip stuck out and her chocolate brown eyes narrowed as she stepped back. Looking past Artie as if she weren't even there, she stepped forward again, colliding with Artie and bumping her a couple of steps up the aisle.

Artie gritted her teeth, lowered her head, and forged forward like a mule throwing itself into its collar. Her shoulder struck Sarah Jane hard in the chest, and the girl grunted. It was a ladylike grunt, but the way she pushed back at Artie was not genteel. Shoulder to shoulder the two leaned, each shoving the other in the opposite direction. Sarah Jane's breath was coming in little, indignant snorts.

All at once it struck Artie as funny—the two of them looking for all the world like two old bulls pushing each other around in a pasture. So she stepped to one side. But when Artie stopped pushing, Sarah Jane catapulted forward two or three stumbling steps before catching herself. Artie didn't even look around to give Sarah Jane the satisfaction of an audience, and she advanced to the doorway.

Pausing there a minute to gaze out at the green and blue world, she drank in the smell of damp earth and budding trees. Just as she was about to step off the threshold, something slammed her between the shoulder blades. With a wild circling of her arms, she tried to regain her balance, teetered on the edge for one long moment, then staggered down the steps like a wounded cow. She whipped around as a dingy pink ruffle disappeared through the door.

Chapter Two

Sarah Jane Bratcher acted as if she owned the world, Artie thought. It was tempting to lie in wait for her and pay her back for the push, but before Artie could plan anything, Ballard came around the corner of the schoolhouse.

"Hey, Art. Ready to go?" His gangly frame was too tall for his faded blue overalls, and his bony face wore a merry grin.

"Yeah, I'm ready." Artie glared at the empty doorway of the schoolhouse, then she and her brother began the long walk home. Once the school was out of sight, she put Sarah Jane out of her mind. "Aren't you glad tomorrow's Saturday?" she asked

Ballard. "Maybe we can rig up that telephone thing you were tellin' me about, with the cans and string."

"I forgot to tell you—Dad and me are going to Leitchfield to see someone about a foxhound." Ballard looked embarrassed.

Artie's stomach knotted up. More often than not her dad would just close the door of his watch and gun repair shop in Caneyville, hang up a sign, and be gone. If he wasn't running his hounds across the country trying to scare up some poor fox or coon to kill, he was visiting somebody or off trading one thing for another—never anything they could really use, as far as she could tell. That meant empty cupboards at home.

And if he was gone on Saturday, who would plow the garden? For weeks Dad had been saying he'd get to it. Already it was late to be planting cold-weather crops like onions, cabbage, and such. Heaven knows they needed all the extra food a garden would produce.

Why didn't Mom insist that Dad ready the ground? Artie knew the answer even as she asked the question—because Mom never risked making Dad mad.

Of course Ballard could plow it, but he never did anything with a mule unless forced to. Besides, he was going to be gone too. Maybe she'd just borrow Grandpa's mule and plow that garden herself. Surprise Dad and please Mom at the same time. Artie had only plowed two rows in her life, and those with Grandpa helping, but it couldn't be that hard.

"What time you goin' to leave?" she asked.

"Dad wants to make an early start," Ballard said. "Uncle Arnold is meetin' us at the top of Buck Creek Hill with his truck at sunup."

She'd do it. If she brought the mule down to the garden right after Dad and Ballard left, she'd have the plowing done in a couple of hours and the mule back in its barn before Mom even realized she'd been gone.

Toiling up long, steep Buck Creek Hill, they followed the dirt road. The walk home from school took nearly an hour, and her stomach always felt so achingly empty by this time of afternoon. Today was no exception. The fried potato and biscuit sandwich she'd had at lunch seemed like forever ago. Yet somehow with the bursting of spring, Artie didn't mind the journey as much as usual.

A group of mailboxes at the crossroad marked the halfway point. From there, Artie could see the roof of Grandpa's place off to the north, and the mounded hill that hid her own house from sight.

When they reached Grandpa Wilson's house, she said, "Go on ahead, Bal. I've got to ask Grandpa something. Be down directly."

"I'm not in no hurry," he said, leaning on the fence there by Grandma's garden. "I'll wait for you, Sis."

Artie worked out the details about borrowing the mule with her grandpa, and soon she and Ballard were striding down the hill. At the bottom, they crossed Big Branch. The creek trickled over its limestone bed and meandered north to where the Wilsons drew their drinking water from a spring near a cavelike overhang.

Partly up the next slope, behind a huddle of black walnut trees, perched a three-room house. A porch stretched across the length of the front, supported beneath by stacks of field rock. Darkness gaped

groundhog—deer were getting hard to come by. Artie set their lunch bucket on the oak slab table and followed Ballard in to see their mother.

Mom was propped up against some pillows. She seemed too small for the bed, and gray shadows showed clearly under her blue eyes. Her voice was low as she asked, "Have a good day?"

"Pretty good," Artie said. She hesitated, then decided against telling of Sarah Jane's hatefulness.

The round mound of baby in her mom's belly raised the patchwork quilt like a Kentucky hill. Just a few more weeks to go.

"Did you sit outside today, Mom?" Ballard asked.

"Yeah," Mom said. "The sun was so warm. I was out near an hour. Perked me up a lot."

"You do sound a might stronger, Mom," Artie said. "And it smells like you started dinner."

"Yes, possum's on t'stove, Artie," Mom said. "I figgered you'd make us some cornbread with the last o' the cornmeal. That'd be good with sorghum. Dad should be home 'long about dark."

The last of the cornmeal. And it wasn't likely that Dad would bring more tonight. But Mom always made it look like they had plenty of food when Dad came home. He probably had no idea how hungry his family was, nor how low supplies were most of the time, because Mom covered up their lack. Wouldn't it be better to let him see how very little they had in the cupboards, and to tell him how often they had to "borrow" something from Grandma?

Artie hurried to do her chores before she made the cornbread. She gathered the eggs in the chicken house, making sure the hens had food and water. Ballard was out splitting firewood for the next day. Artie waved to him as she set out to find Ol' Friendly, their brindle cow, and drive her to the narrow two-stall barn for the night's milking.

Tonight there was no grain to feed the rangy cow and Friendly moved restlessly. *Fwish, chish, fwish, chish*—the milk sang into the tin bucket in a steady rhythm, making a layer of foam like a fluffy cloud.

Artie didn't mind milking. There was something soothing about it, except during winter when the cold bit through her thin coat and gnawed at her toes through the holes in her shoes. Or when a mucky cow's tail, greeny brown from a recent bath in mud and manure, whacked her upside the head.

Careful to milk out the last creamy drops, Artie skillfully stripped the teats. If she left too much milk in the cow's bag, the animal would dry up before she ought to. That would leave the family without milk longer than the usual two or three months before coming fresh again after calving. Already Friendly's milk supply was dwindling, though her calf wasn't due until July. With food so hard to come by, they would sure miss the milk and butter come summer.

Artie shut Friendly up in the barn so she wouldn't have to go traipsing around through dew and fog searching for an unwilling cow before the morning milking. After she forked enough hay to the cow to last through the night, she carried the foamy milk to the kitchen. She strained it through a clean cloth to filter out any bits of grass or dust that might have fallen from the cow's belly, then she set it in the coolest corner of the kitchen. The cream should rise by morning, and she or Mom would skim it and make butter.

Artie sighed as she began preparing the corn-bread. She lit the kitchen lamp and placed it on the table as the weak spring sun lost its evening battle with darkness. Everyone in Louisville must have electricity, maybe even an icebox or one of those electric refrigerators. Even in Caneyville some houses had electricity now.

The hounds erupted from under the porch with wild bayings and barkings, interrupting her thoughts. Dad must be home from Caneyville—at least he wasn't as late as usual.

Mixed feelings washed over her. It was as if two people argued in her mind, one saying, "Wonder if he earned any money today, or just had fun." The other, "Shame on you, of course he earned some-thing. And if he didn't, surely there was a good rea-son." To which the first voice would reply, "Good reasons don't put food on the table."

Caught between these voices, Artie did not drop everything to run and greet her father as she used to when she was younger. Instead she checked the corn-bread browning in the oven and lifted the big pot of possum stew to the table. As she turned back around, she collided with her father's broad chest. "Smells good in here, Artie-gal," he said, and his voice was a mixture of laughter and honey. He was like a fresh wind blowing. Everything in the small room looked brighter, more alive when Dad was there. He was almost too full of life to be bound by four walls—like a wild horse with head high, tail and mane flowing out behind, ready to race the wind. His black hair glinted in the lamplight, and his eyes were blue as a summer sky. Grandma always said, "My son Reason could charm the skin right off a snake and leave the poor thing smilin' in the dirt and a-thankin' him for the favor."

"Hello, everybody," Dad boomed as he took his chair at the table. "Smells like supper's a-waitin' for someone to eat it." His voice was mellow and deep, like coffee with thick cream and sugar—warm and full-bodied. "Where's my lovely wife this fine evening?"

Mom came into the kitchen from her bed in the parlor, smiling and tucking a wisp of brown hair behind her ear. Ballard laid aside the automobile magazine he'd borrowed from the mechanic shop in town and took his place opposite Artie. It was good to have everyone home. After Mom said a blessing on the food, they all ate possum and cornbread by the glow of the kerosene lamp.

Stirring a chunk of butter into the dark pool of sorghum molasses on her plate, Artie whipped it into a creamy tan and spooned it onto the hot cornbread. It may have been made with the last of the cornmeal, but it sure tasted good.

"Looks like Will Bratcher's got a new team o' horses," Dad said. "Matched grays and mighty showy. Saw 'em turnin' in at his house."

Sarah Jane's father had a big house, lots of land, horses, mules, and only one child to lavish everything on, when all Artie's pap had was a bunch of coon- and foxhounds, a tiny farm, a sick wife, and hungry kids. The Bratchers even had a 1928 Roadster. Why should they now have a matched team of horses when Artie's family always had to borrow Grandpa's mule, or pay or trade with someone to take them somewhere? It embarrassed Artie just to think about it.

"Couldn't we get a horse, Dad? A nice horse?"

"Had a nice horse once, Artie-gal. Real nice black saddle mare that I traded to yer grandpa for these twenty-five acres."

"But don't you want a horse again?" Artie wheedled.

Reason Wilson's face clouded over like a sudden thunderstorm. "Got too many mouths to feed as it is," he said, his words short and clipped. "Couldn't keep a pleasure horse even if it were given to me with a bow around its neck. Doin' my best to come up with a mule to work the fields come summer."

Artie hardly breathed, staring at her plate, while the possum stew churned in her stomach. What did Dad mean by "too many mouths"? Was he referring to the new baby, or to all of them? Probably all of them. Hard to run hounds and be gone for days at a time like before he was married, now he'd got young 'uns. Still, it wasn't as if Mom had gotten this baby, Ballard, Liddie, or her out of the Sears and Roebuck catalog without checking with Dad first. If he hadn't wanted kids, why'd he get married in the first place?

She heard her mother's chair scrape the wood floor. Mom always faded out of the picture when Dad exploded. Artie didn't blame her and tried not to mind. But part of her wished Mom would stay and protect her from the anger, or at least share the weight of it.

"Guess what I heard?" Ballard interrupted her dark thoughts.

"What?" Artie asked. She knew what Ballard was doing. They had danced this dance many times, seeking to ease their father out of a foul mood and bring the smile back into his eyes.

"President Hoover says the Depression is ending. Prices are up."

"Says who?" Dad growled. He was hunched over his plate, his black brows pulled down in a heavy frown.

"Richard King. You know—his dad owns the drugstore in Caneyville."

Some of the frown wrinkles left Dad's face. "Be a thousand wonders if it were over so easy," he said. "Farmers 'round these parts has been in a depression for nigh on to ten years. It keeps up much longer and we'll lose the shirts on our backs. I'm satisfied we ain't seen the last of it yet."

He was talking. That was a good sign.

Ballard asked questions in the right places and Artie made sure Dad's cup and plate were kept full. Soon, except for her mother's empty chair and the tightness in Artie's chest, it seemed as if the episode had never happened. She took another bite of cornbread, swallowing around the lessening lump in her throat, and listened to Dad and Ballard plan their Saturday.

Now that the storm was over, Mom came out of the bedroom and sat in her rocker in the cramped living room. "Reason?" Mom said as he stood up from the table. "Will you play the fiddle tonight?"

"Want a little song and dance, eh, Katie?" he teased, and did a couple of fancy dance steps.

Mom smiled. "I just think it'd sound real nice this evening, Reason, if ya don't mind."

Dad bent over, kissed the top of her head, and said, "Anything for my girlie."

Mom's heart shone out through her eyes, love and hurt and hope all wrapped up together, and Artie couldn't bear to look on it long.

Dad took his fiddle from the case, tightened the hair on the bow, and tuned the strings. "What'll it be, ladies and gentleman?" he asked with a flourish of the bow.

"How 'bout 'Arkansas Traveler'?" Ballard suggested. "Or maybe 'My Old Kentucky Home'?"

The music wound in and out of the corners of the house and filled the whole world with the rollicking, lilting, and sometimes haunting tunes. Dad's old violin seemed to sing under his flying fingers. Artie's struggles, the drudgery of chores, and her deep desire to go places in life faded for a while. Sometimes when listening to Dad play, she felt as if her soul would float away on a river of song.

He swung into a gay song about banjos and wagons and *"don't you cry for me."* In spite of herself, Artie found her toe tapping and her heart lifting. She wished she could play music like her dad did. But music didn't flow from her. It kind of dripped. Straggled. Limped. Artie pulled her knees up to her chin and let the notes wash over her. No one in the whole of Grayson County could play like Dad could.

In bed that night, Artie pondered her plans to plow the garden the next morning. The moaning whistle of a freight train called to her as it crossed Caney Creek, bound for Caneyville, Leitchfield, Louisville, and beyond. She pictured the big iron wheels carrying her a world away from life in the backwoods of Kentucky. Pulling the quilt up to her chin, Artie blinked back tears.

Chapter Three

The next morning found Artie in the dimness of her grandfather's barn. She took the padded leather collar from where it hung on the wall and slipped into the stall with Grandpa's mule. Reaching up, she slid the collar onto the mule's neck, fumbling to find the buckles. The big animal leaned against Artie like a lazy man in a doorway.

"Stand up there, you ol' fleabag!" Artie said, digging her shoulder into the mule's ribs. Pansy flipped her long ears back and forth and shifted her feet. Artie finished buckling the collar on, making sure it fit snugly so no sores would rub on the mule's neck. Lifting the leather harness from the pegs where it hung on the barn wall, she approached Pansy from the off, or left, side. The furry back was level with the top of her head, so she dragged an old bucket over to stand on in order to heave the harness up and settle it in place.

There. Now to fasten the breeching behind Pansy's back legs to keep the harness from slipping forward. Then she'd buckle the rest of the straps and the mule would be all hooked up. It looked so easy when Dad or Grandpa did it. Whoever thought it could be such a process? Even in the coolness of the early April morning, and though her bare feet were wet and cold from the heavy dew she'd walked through, sweat beaded up on her forehead.

Dawn was still painting the east in rosy colors when she led the harnessed mule out of Grandpa's barn and started down the hill for home. So far, so good.

"Good girl, Pansy," Artie said, patting the animal. The mule was iron gray in the legs and nicely dappled through the body, her huge head light-colored and stippled with darker gray.

Pansy swiveled her ears this way and that, her

eyes looking wise behind the blinds of her bridle. Gazing off over the rolling, wooded country, Artie could see drifts of fog hanging in the hollows, and an early morning haze softening the trees on the horizon. The cool air that washed over her face like fresh water was full of tree scents and a hint of rain.

Down the hill and across Big Branch, Artie led the mule to where Dad's walking plow leaned against their barn. After some pushing and tugging, she managed to hitch Pansy to it.

"Giddap."

Pansy swung her big head around as if to say, "Are you serious?" Her neat little nose quivered a little, like she was trying not to smile.

"Get up there, Pansy," Artie said in a louder voice. Grandpa always said mules were smarter than horses, but you had to let them know you were in charge or they wouldn't mind any better than a spoiled kid. The problem was, Artie didn't feel very in charge.

"Come on, mule," she said, a little more forcefully and smacked the reins on the gray back. Pansy stepped out and Artie swelled with pride. She was doing it. Everything was going according to plan.

But five steps later she discovered the challenge in guiding a mule and steering a plow at the same time. If she let go of the plow handles to steer the mule, the plow fell over; and if she dropped the reins to steady the plow, Pansy wandered off course or stopped in her tracks. Dad always hung the reins over his shoulder and held the plow handles with his hands, but she'd never watched him get from barn to field.

"Whoa."

Pansy stopped. After consideration, Artie decided she'd just drag the plow on its side until she reached the garden. But as the plow bounced and skidded along the rocky yard it left a raw, red gash in greening weeds. So much for surprise. Might as well have posted a sign for Dad. He'd see that drag mark the moment he got home.

She finally managed to position the plow at the foot of the garden. Throwing the reins over her shoulder like Dad did, she grabbed hold of the wooden handles and clucked to the mule. Pansy looked around again, but didn't move.

"Giddap, Pansy!" Artie said with as much force as she could. The mule stood like a furry statue, staring off into the distance. Artie gritted her teeth. How was she supposed to snap the reins and hold the plow at the same time? She snatched the leather straps from her shoulder and slapped them down hard on the mule's back.

Pansy surged forward, and the plow leaped from its place, skidding several feet before Artie could get her hands back on the handles and set the point of the plowshare into the dirt. There. The rust-colored soil rolled away from the steel of the plowshare in a neat furrow. Copacetic.

Artie whistled as she stepped along behind the plow. Just like a pioneer, she thought.

When they had plowed the length of the garden, Artie stopped, turned, then set the plowshare into the new furrow at a right angle to cut a furrow across the end.

"Giddap."

Pansy didn't move.

Artie stomped and bruised her foot on a sharp stone. "Giddap, you dumb ol' mule!" she shouted, and snapped the reins as hard as she could.

Pansy shot forward, and the plow flipped out of

Artie's hands, falling on its side and skidding along the ground.

"Whoa! *Whoa,* mule!" Artie yelled, pulling back on the reins. Now how was she supposed to back up this hunk of metal and wood so there wouldn't be a big, unplowed gap? Suddenly the garden looked huge. Tears of frustration welled up. Maybe she should just take Pansy home and go do the laundry, which was waiting for her. Nobody told her to plow this old garden, anyway. It wasn't her responsibility. It was her dad's. He should have been home plowing, not running off across the county after some mangy hound. She'd show him. She'd turn the soil in this old garden if it killed her.

Twenty minutes later, Artie had the plow repositioned. Sweat dripped off her forehead, stinging her eyes. She bared her teeth like a cornered coon. "Giddap!"

Perhaps Pansy detected a certain no-nonsense tone to Artie's voice, for this time there was no turning of the head, no standing like a rock. The mule threw her big shoulders into the collar and pulled.

They marched straight across the end and before

long were plowing down the far side, neat and clean. Artie made the turn at the next corner without too much difficulty, and met up with the first furrow she had made, making a rectangle frame around the garden plot. The longer she plowed, the better she got, and with each successive round, the fire of anger faded. But the joy of the gift she had wanted to give her parents lay tarnished in the ashes.

It was nearly noon before she unhitched the plow and looped the reins up on the harness hames in order to lead Pansy home. The garden lay brown-red and rich, open to the sun, ready to seed.

Once in Grandpa's barn, she made quick work of unharnessing. After watering Pansy and leaving her to eat, Artie gave her one last pat. "Thanks for your help."

Grandma's house wasn't fancy, but it always seemed to welcome Artie with open arms. A deep, broad porch stretched across the front, with a swing hanging on one end where Grandma liked to sit and shell peas or snap beans in the summer or just enjoy the long, lazy afternoons.

In summertime, blue-flowered morning glory

vines would wind their way up the posts that supported the porch roof, and Grandma usually had some pink Missouri primrose blooming in an old bucket under the windows.

Artie stuck her head inside the door. "Grandma?"

"Right here, Artie. How'd the plowin' go?"

Artie melted into a chair. "Got it done."

Grandma straightened from where she had been stirring a pot over the open fire on the hearth. She had a wood cookstove, but she preferred cooking over the fireplace, like she'd grown up doing. She always made her cornbread in a Dutch oven that sat on the ashes. She would shovel hot coals on the lid to give an even heat from top and bottom. The thought of the brown-crusted, mealy yellow bread made Artie's mouth water.

"Any problems?"

"Took me awhile to figure out how to drive and plow at the same time. But it looks real good."

Grandma smiled. "You could do about anything you put yer mind to, girl." She passed Artie a wedge of buttered cornbread.

"Hmmm."

"Ain't you happy?" Grandma's knowing eye was on her.

Artie shrugged.

Grandma eased her bulk into the chair next to Artie. "I'll tell you the truth. Though he's my own son, I don't know why yer pap don't do more by you. I'm plumb put out with him over that. Fact is, Grandpa is of a mind to disown him, and if it weren't for yer mom and you kids, we wouldn't give him one more cup of cornmeal and that's a fact." She sighed. "God knows we tried to raise him right."

The silence grew long. At last Artie said, "Seems like God isn't fair sometimes."

"Well, I know what you mean," Grandma said, "but I suppose we just got to let God be God. The Good Book says that God's ways ain't man's ways." She sighed again. "I reckon there's a heap of things we don't see God's way."

"Maybe," Artie said. She munched her way through another piece of cornbread.

"How's school goin' fer ya? How do ya like yer new teacher?"

"Oh, I like her fine, but I miss my old teacher a

lot." How could Artie put into words what an empty place Miss Meyers had left behind?

Thinking of her teachers reminded Artie of the contest. "Oh, Grandma, guess what? There's an essay contest for the schools in our area and the winner gets a twenty-five-dollar savings bond to use to go to high school!"

"What ya want to go to high school for?" Grandma asked. "Ain't none of yer folks ever made it as far in school as you and Ballard has already. Cain't see it hurt us none."

"Don't you ever want to see the world outside of here, Grandma?"

Grandma Wilson's blue eyes softened. "Yeah, I reckon I did, when I was yer age. Wanted to finish out my schooling, anyway. But after Mom died I sorta gave up on that. Then I up and married yer grandpa and started a family of my own and never gave it no more thought."

"Do you think I can win?"

Grandma nodded. "Well, if anyone can win that essay contest, you can. Yer smart as a whip."

Artie grinned. "We have to write about our

heritage," she said. "We have to find interesting stories about our ancestors and show how they helped make us who we are today. Do you know any interesting stories I can tell?"

Grandma poured Artie a glass of buttermilk. "Well, let's see. Yer family goes clear back to the colonists, before the Revolutionary War. One of yer great-great—I don't know how many greats—grandfathers fought in the battle of Bunker Hill. We got settlers and pioneers all the way back to the beginning of our country. Determined folk. Solid." Grandma seemed to be looking far away.

Settlers didn't sound very exciting compared to plantation owners. "But how does that make me who I am?"

Grandma led the way out to the porch swing. Settling comfortably, she patted the seat beside her. Artie sat, her toes just touching the porch floor.

"Well, girl," Grandma began, "I seen that same determination in you from the day you was borned."

Artie knew the story of her birth, but she'd never heard it started that way. "Like how?" she asked.

"January 18, 1918, it was, and the hardest winter

we'd had since time out of mind. Snow was so high you could drive a wagon clean over the fences. Never seen the like afore ner since."

Artie tried to picture that much snow.

"Yer mom was sick with the consumption back then too—real sick—and it looked like she'd die any day. The doctor done told her she shouldn't go havin' no more babies, but she was lookin' forward to yer birth anyways. Yer uncle John fetched the doctor and he like to froze to death on the way. Doc Collins, he left his horse and rig at our house and walked on down to yer mom. I come down with him."

"But how did this make me—"

"I'm gettin' there," Grandma said. "The house were so cold, we jist kept heapin' the logs on, but the heat never reached the corners. Long about mornin' you was borned, but yer ma was so bad off the doctor just handed you to me to take care of."

Artie scooted closer.

"Yep, I cleaned you up and wrapped you warm, but yer ma couldn't feed you, she was that sick. So I made you a little teat out of butter and sugar in the corner of a rag. You sucked that, and it kept you alive. I didn't think you'd make it, you was that small and it were so cold. But you never give in. Somehow you hung in there till yer mom started to pull around and was able to nurse you. It musta been that determination, that fight you inherited."

Grandma's words spread warmth in Artie's chest. The thought fascinated her—linked to ancestors by a thread of determination.

"Anything else?" she asked.

"Well, there was that time when you was about two years old. You and Ballard come down with scarlet fever. You was so sick, we thought you died, so we laid you off to the side to take care of later."

This story was new to Artie.

"Yeah, laid you off to the side and after a bit yer mom looked up and saw you move. Bless yer little heart, you was determined to live. Made me feel bad, that we had give up on you." Grandma sighed.

"That's all right, Grandma," Artie said. "Here I am, big and healthy. Well, healthy anyway, if not big."

"So you are," Grandma said. "Can you see how you musta taken after those ancestors?"

"I suppose so," Artie said. "But it's not as exciting as inheriting riches."

"Artesia May Wilson." Grandma stopped swinging. "Anybody can get money. But the will to fight and the gumption to make yer way in life is something money cain't buy."

Late that afternoon as the sun spread its fiery blanket of orange over the western sky, the dogs exploded from under the porch and barreled down the slope as Dad and Ballard came walking up the long driveway across the hollow. A new hound, big and red, danced around their feet. Ballard said something to Dad, who burst into laughter and whacked Ballard on the back.

The memory of her mother's pleasure over the garden still fresh upon her, Artie waited until they shut the new hound up in the barn, then went to meet them.

"Did you see my new dog, Artie-gal?" Dad's dimples showed deep. "Got a nose on him that'll have the rest of the hounds apologizing. Cain't wait to run him after some ornery old coon."

"Come see my surprise, Dad," she said, tugging on his arm, and Ballard followed.

The garden lay like a splash of brown velvet on the tangled yellow grass of the clearing behind the house. Her father stood dead still and his eyes went from sky blue to the color of a winter storm.

"I was goin' to get to it," he said. Then he turned on his heel and stalked off.

Ballard wouldn't meet her eyes. "What'd I do wrong, Bal? Wasn't it a good surprise?"

Her brother picked up a rock and threw it as hard as he could. "You didn't do nothin' wrong, Art," he said. "Nothin' at all." He turned and looked at her. "Don't pay Dad no mind. It was a good surprise."

Artie nodded.

Ballard tweaked her hair. "If I was you, Art, I'd be a might more cautious about showin' what a good job of plowin' I could do. You might end up havin' to do a lot of it!"

Artie smiled her thanks.

Chapter Four

Monday morning, April 14, 1930. Artie slumped low in her seat. Usually she loved writing things, but today the blank paper on her desk stared up at her as she labored on the first sentence of her essay. She finally wrote, "My Heritage, by Artesia May Wilson." It had an impressive look. Squeezing her eyes shut, she tried to re-create the feeling that had come over her Saturday on Grandma's porch.

Taking care to leave a nice margin on the left and indent her first word, she wrote, "A heritage is more than an inheritance of land or money." And there she stuck. Finally, she raised her hand. "Miss Small?"

"Yes, Artie?"

"I can't think of what to write for my essay paper." Sighs from other students indicated they were having the same trouble.

"All right," Miss Small said. "Maybe someone can share something about his family to stir some creative ideas. Does anyone want to volunteer?"

It appeared that everyone was fresh out of ideas. Except for Sarah Jane Bratcher. She had been unusually quiet all morning, but now she waved her hand with energy.

"Yes, Sarah?" Miss Small said.

"I found out some more very interesting facts about my family that I could tell everybody." Sarah Jane smiled like a queen.

"That would be nice, Sarah," Miss Small said. The chorus of moans brought Miss Small's eyebrows down sternly.

Sarah Jane began. "As I told you on Friday, my ancestors were plantation owners in the South. Rich plantation owners."

Artie snorted.

Sarah Jane glared at Artie, then continued. "But I found out that before they were plantation owners, they owned a huge estate in England. In fact, we are related to Lord William Bratcher of Coningsdale, England." She beamed at everyone, then plumped down into her seat with a self-satisfied air.

"Thank you, Sarah. I can see you will have plenty of material to write about," Miss Small said. "Has anyone else thought of anything they might be able to share?" She looked around in an expectant manner. "Yes, Ballard. Do you have something?"

Ballard? Artie resisted the impulse to turn around and stare at him. What did he know that she didn't?

"Yep," Ballard drawled. "Dad was a-tellin' me that we had quite a character in our lineup."

Artie shrank low in her chair. Oh, Ballard, please, please don't tell anything embarrassing. And don't talk so—so backwoods, either. Artie could feel her face getting red. Ever since Miss Meyers had been their teacher, she'd tried so hard to talk correctly, but Ballard didn't seem to care what he sounded like.

"Go ahead, Ballard," Miss Small urged.

"Well, it was in 1864. My great-grandma—Emily Yager Wilson—she had three children and then her husband up an' died of measles in the Civil War, 'bout five months afore my grandpa was borned."

Borned. Ballard could talk better than that.

"Anyways, Great-Grandma was out in her yard gathering stove wood, when up rides a man on a fine black horse. This here man was named Mason Embry, and he said, 'Madam, my wife has died, leavin' me with five children. I'm a-needin' a new wife. Throw down your wood and turn around so's I can look you over.'"

Artie made a face. If that had been her, she'd have thrown the wood at that Mason Embry instead.

"So she dropped her wood and turned around, and the man said, 'You'll do.' He never even got down offen his horse. Guess they were both glad to have a father and mother to their kids, 'cause she done married him, and my grandpa was born that December. They went on to have a fine life together and seven more kids."

See, he knows it's supposed to be *born,* not *borned.* Artie could have kicked her brother. Every time Ballard used poor grammar, Sarah Jane would give a ladylike jump, as if she was shocked to hear such language. It looked like she had the twitch.

"Is that all, Ballard?" Miss Small asked.

"Well, there's actually a lot more," Ballard said, "But I'll just share another real interestin' fact, if that's all right."

"Yes, you may go ahead." Miss Small nodded. Artie sank lower in her seat.

Ballard grinned. "Well, this here Mason Embry was a right smart businessman, made lots o' money. But he didn't trust banks, so he always had people pay him in gold or silver. Then he'd take that cash and head out into the woods. Little bit later, here he'd come back without no money. My great-grandma, she tried to follow him to see where he was a-buryin' it, but he give her the slip ever time."

Ballard seemed to be enjoying his role as entertainer. "Now Great-Grandpa was a big one for runnin' his dogs, and one hot summer day toward the end of August, his hounds run an animal to ground under a big tree root. So Great-Grandpa, he took to diggin' that varmint out. Guess he dug so hard he got overhet and died. Heat stroke, the doctors called it. It all happened so fast that Great-Grandma never thought to ask about where he'd hid the money. My dad supposes it's still out there in my grandpa's woods under some tree or other, just waitin' for someone to find it."

The classroom was as quiet as if it were deserted. Even Sarah Jane stared at Ballard. Artie forgot her embarrassment over her brother's grammar. A fortune buried in the woods, and she never knew it? Here they were in a drafty house on a tiny farm with hardly anything to their name—to say nothing of the Depression and Dad barely keeping food on the table—while all this time there was money for the finding?

School suddenly seemed endless. She had to get out there and start digging.

At lunchtime, students surrounded Ballard, wanting to hear more of his stories. Artie tried to pull him off by himself to persuade him not to give out any more secrets about the possible fortune in Grandpa's woods, but she couldn't get him to leave his admirers. It wasn't until they were on their way home that she was able to question him and tell him of her Great Plan.

"Ballard," Artie whispered. "How in the world did you find out all that stuff about Mason Embry?"

"Dad and Uncle Arnold told me Saturday when we were gettin' the new dog."

"Shhh," Artie hissed. "Not so loud. I've got an idea."

Ballard glanced over his shoulder, pretending that they might be followed, and whispered, "Let me guess—you want to dig up Mason Embry's treasure, right?"

"It's not funny." Artie aimed a halfhearted kick at her brother. "I'm serious. If we find that treasure, we could maybe have plenty of food, a new house, horses—even a car." She couldn't care less about a car, except for the look on Sarah Jane's face as they drove by, but Artie knew that Ballard loved cars and would give about anything to get one.

Sure enough, Ballard quit fooling around. "So what's your plan?"

"It would help if we knew in which direction Great-Grandpa used to go when he went to bury his money. We'll need some kind of a system, so we're not digging all over the place. Maybe sorta map out the likely spots and try them first." Artie tingled with excitement.

"We'll have to do our chores in a hurry each day when we get home from school, then put in an hour or two of digging," she continued. "Most likely we'll have to spell each other, and not be away from the house at the same time. I don't think Mom will mind us looking for the money as long as we get our work done." She felt quite virtuous as she said this. "I'll dig first."

They planned and spent the money several times over before they reached home. Artie didn't want to wait to hear if Mom knew the direction to go—she did her chores with more speed than thoroughness, grabbed some dried apples to eat and a shovel to dig with, and was soon deep into the greening woods.

"Let's see," she said out loud. "He wouldn't have buried it next to a stream, in case it washed away. Probably in a cave or at the foot of some big tree—" Artie selected the biggest tree she could see and set to work. And work it was. Roots and rocks slowed her progress, and it took half an hour to excavate a hole not quite a foot deep.

"Whew." She wiped her forehead. Grandpa's woods were sure a lot bigger than she remembered. She decided to try a different spot, and so, crossing a small creek, she came upon an open glade with a ring of trees in an almost perfect circle. Her heart beat faster.

But an hour and several holes later, Artie threw down her shovel. Even if the money was still somewhere about, how could they ever hope to stumble on it? She could dig a thousand holes and be no closer to finding it. Sighing, she shouldered her shovel once again and turned to go, then stopped. Something had fluttered at the edge of the clearing. Was it a deer? No, there it was again—something yellow as butter, moving, stopping, and moving again. Artie squinted against the dropping sun of late afternoon and realized she was staring at Sarah Jane Bratcher.

In *Grandpa's* woods? Heat crept up Artie's neck as she watched Sarah Jane take a shovel from her shoulder and begin to dig at the base of a big oak tree.

"Hey, you! Sarah Jane!" Artie charged toward her classmate.

The girl whipped around and hid the shovel behind her back. "Shame on you, Artie Wilson, for spying on me," she said. Pink burned on her round cheeks.

"I wasn't spying. I was exploring *my* grandpa's woods," Artie said pointedly, hiding her own shovel. "You're trespassing. And what are you doing with that shovel?"

Sarah Jane seemed at a momentary loss for words. "I'm a—I'm—"

"I know what you're doing," Artie accused. "You're digging for old Mason Embry's buried gold."

Sarah Jane tossed her head, flipping her long black curls behind her plump shoulders. Her brown eyes narrowed. "Well, so what if I am? That's what you're doing too, isn't it?" She took her shovel from behind her back and stuck it into the hole she had started.

It was Artie's turn to search for words. "But it belongs to *my* ancestor, so it belongs to *my* family. Your father has plenty of money already, what with your English ancestors and their big estate. You're the one with the big house and the hired help. My dad said your father just got a new matched pair of horses."

Sarah Jane dropped her gaze and poked the dirt with her shovel. "What do you know, Artie Wilson? I can dig wherever I want to and you can't stop me." When she looked up again, Artie was taken aback to see tears in her eyes.

"Well, if you want to dig, go dig on your own land," Artie said, but in the face of Sarah Jane's distress, the words kind of dribbled out. "This here woods is ours."

Sarah Jane spun on her heel and stalked off toward Bratcher land.

Chapter Five

At school the next day, Artie stole glances at Sarah Jane, looking for a hint of their encounter in the woods. However, Sarah Jane avoided Artie's eyes and acted the same as always, handing in her neat, always correct schoolwork and keeping her area in order.

The students grouped around Ballard at noontime, begging to hear more about his exciting ancestors. Sarah Jane watched him like a bird caught in a snake's hypnotic gaze.

Artie didn't have time to think about Sarah Jane for very long. Writing the heritage paper was harder than she'd thought. Her first sentence seemed fine—*A heritage is more than an inheritance of land or money.* But more words were hard to find.

"My heritage is invisible," she wrote. No. How about, "My heritage is a long one?" Definitely no. She leaned over and whispered to Eula, "I'm glad we've got till next month to write this—I'm goin' to need every day of it."

Each night that week after school, once Artie did her chores, she took her shovel and dug a few more holes in the floor of the forest. By the time Ballard joined her on Friday, she was beginning to think she'd be better off coming up with some other plan to earn money. Together they searched for likely spots where a suspicious man might have hidden his riches. As they dug here and there, they came across holes neither had made.

"Where do you suppose these came from?" Ballard asked.

"Could be that Sarah Jane Bratcher. I caught her sneakin' around here the other day." Artie sniffed. "Don't know why she wants more money, the greedy thing."

"Aw, Artie. You've just got it in for her. She's not that bad of a kid, far's I can see, outside of bein' a bit on the braggy side."

"A bit?" Artie snorted.

Ballard grinned. "She's really pretty nice with everybody else. You two just rub each other the wrong way, I guess."

"Yeah, I guess."

Ballard leaned on his shovel. "Any idea what's for supper?"

Artie leaned on hers. "I forgot—Mom said you're supposed to go borrow some cornmeal from Grandma. Again."

"How'd Mom look to you today?" Ballard asked.

"Tired."

Mom stayed in bed more and more, though she coughed less than she used to, and said she felt good. Some people did recover from TB, but more did not. Tuberculosis was tricky that way.

But Mom had said, "I can't die. I gotta live, else you and Ballard will get farmed out to relatives. Fact is, ol' Aunt Liz down in Butler County has spoke for you already. Can't let that happen."

Aunt Liz! "I wouldn't live with that old slave driver," Artie had protested. "I'd run away. Oh, Mom, you just got to get well."

"I will, child. I will," Mom had said. "I'm takin' it easy, givin' these lungs time to heal. I'm goin' to see my young'uns grown. I'm prayin', and I'm thinkin' God's goin' to make me well."

Remembering that conversation, Artie shuddered. "Ballard? I'm going to see how Mom is doing. Do you mind?"

Ballard stuck his shovel into the ground. "Naw, that'd be fine. I'll dig a bit longer, then go get the cornmeal from Grandma."

Artie sprinted for home. She left her shovel in the barn as she passed by and moments later stood panting in the quietness of her mother's room.

"Hi, Mom."

"Hello, Artie-girl. What you been up to?"

Artie recounted their lack of progress, to which her mother replied, "Wish I could tell ya where to look. Yet dad keeps his eyes open evertime he walks the woods; hasn't found it yet. That money'd come in right handy 'long about now." Her pale face must have been pretty at one time, with its blue eyes and soft, brown hair, but her fifteen-year battle with tuberculosis had made her look like an old woman—sunken cheeks, thin neck, worry lines—though she was only thirty-eight years old.

"Actually, I'm beginning to think that there's not much point in trying to find that buried treasure," Artie said. "I could dig over the whole woods and never find the right spot. Now I'm thinking about digging sassafras and mayapples, like Dad says the old-timers did. It's a little late in spring to be digging May roots but I could still try. The store pays cash money for roots. It wouldn't be much, but it would help some."

"Just don't be eatin' none of it yourself, Artie. Them leaves and roots can be real poisonous if took wrong."

Artie did some quick calculations in her head. She could hold back one cent from every five she earned and start a school fund. It would take a long time, but it would be another two years before she was old enough for high school, anyway. "Maybe I'll start tomorrow, since it's Saturday."

"I was wonderin' if you might like to go with yer dad to pick up Aunt Milly tomorrow," Mom said. "Grandpa got a new mule and he wants Dad to try it out. Milly, she's goin' to come help me sew on your dress for May Meeting. She'll stay on till the baby comes."

"Would I!" Artie hugged her mom. Last time Aunt Milly came, she had shared some of her perfume with Artie and showed her a few chords on the guitar she brought with her. Aunt Milly and Mom seemed to always be giggling over some incident or other from their growing-up years, and Mom perked up so when they were together.

"I can't wait!" Artie said.

But then some of her eagerness drained away. The drive to Ready would take a couple of hours. With Dad still mad about the garden, those would be awfully long hours. He'd hardly spoken to her all week, and never mentioned the plowing at all.

When her dad woke her early the next morning, Artie threw on an old pair of overalls and a patched and faded blue chambray shirt that Ballard had outgrown. She loved wearing something different from her everyday dress. Besides, Liddie said that in Louisville, women were starting to wear slacks. Around Caneyville, only fast women wore slacks. Artie wasn't sure what "fast" meant—something bad, by the tone of voice it was usually said in. She didn't want to be whatever it was, but if they were wearing pants in Louisville, it must be all right and people around these parts just didn't know better.

For breakfast, Artie buttered last night's leftover biscuits (made with Grandma's cornmeal) and rolled them in the newspaper Dad had brought from town last week. As she went out the door, she snatched a parasol of grass green silk that had once been Aunt Milly's.

"And what might you be needing that for?" Dad asked.

"Sun might get too hot for us," Artie answered. She liked the picture of herself sitting high on the wagon seat under the frilly green parasol, nodding to Sarah Jane as they passed by. Elegant. "Besides, I thought Aunt Milly might like to see me using it."

"Well, don't go waving it in front of the mules,"

he said. "That new mule of Grandpa's is as scatty as a barn cat."

Dad checked the mules' harnesses, while Artie clambered to the seat of the spring wagon. Then he jumped up beside her, and they set off up the road in the cool morning fog. The newly leafed trees wore gossamer veils, and birds sang wake-up songs. Off across the creek, the early morning train blew for a crossing—two long wails, one short, and another long. But this time it did not stir the usual longing in Artie, for she was already going somewhere, doing something.

The mules stepped out willingly, their harness clinking, their hooves clumping in rhythm on the dry roadbed. Pansy and Pete. Grandpa had gotten Pete from a stockman just Wednesday of the past week. He was as brown as oak leaves in the fall, a three-year-old horse mule—a male, not a mare mule like Pansy, and green-broke—he'd never plowed and had hardly been in harness. Grandpa would keep him all summer and the stockman would come back in the fall and pick him up. It was sort of a trade. That way Grandpa had the use of a mule all summer,

and by fall the mule would be worth a hundred dollars more to the stockman, because he would be a
trained animal.

Pansy pulled along with her ears pricked forward
and her shoulders well into the collar. Pete's ears
flipped back and forth, and he kept trying to look
around the blinders on his bridle, shying at whatever he managed to see, throwing himself into the
collar, then holding back and being tugged along by
the steady gray mule at his side.

Artie stole a glance at her father. He stared
straight ahead, his brows pulled down and his lips
pursed.

She gathered her courage. "Dad?"

"Yeah?"

"Dad, I'm sorry about plowin' the garden. I just
wanted to give you a surprise. I wasn't meaning to
make you feel bad."

There. The words were out.

Reason Wilson stared off at some spot beyond
Pete's ears, and the silence grew.

Just about the time Artie thought she would

drown in pent-up emotions, her father said, "Used to come this way courtin' yer maw. Pretty road, ain't it?"

He smiled at her, his dimples flashing. Nothing about the garden. Nothing about her apology. But the morning sun seemed suddenly brighter. It warmed her back and filled the world with light.

She sidled closer to him and leaned against his shoulder, feeling the rough fabric of his shirt against her cheek and his arm strong and solid beneath.

After a while, Artie brought out the biscuits. The newsprint left black smudges on their breakfast, but that was nothing unusual. All the students at Buck Creek wrapped their lunches in newspaper, except Sarah Jane.

Artie savored the saltiness of the butter, and the nutty corn taste. She liked wheat biscuits better, but wheat flour was even harder to come by than cornmeal. Besides, corn biscuits tasted mighty nice when her stomach was gnawing at her ribs like a starving hound dog.

Dad whistled a sprightly tune that seemed to charm the birds into accompanying him. He clucked and coaxed Pete into submitting to the harness and settling down to the job at hand. Pride warmed her chest. Her pap was one of the best horse and mule men in the county.

"He jest knows what to do. Ain't no mule can get the best of Reason," Grandpa had said, and Artie agreed. She could see that Pete's antics didn't concern her dad at all.

Artie watched the mules' ears pricking and flopping, listening to the sounds around them. "Dad, what's the difference between mules and horses? I mean, why get a mule when you could have a horse?"

"Depends on what you need 'im for," her father said. "You needin' a plow animal, get yourself a mule. A mule'll outwork just about any horse on hooves. They're tough, sure-footed, usually not as spooky, and they're smarter, too. A mule will slow down if he starts to overheat, where a horse just keeps goin' till he drops in harness. A mule will never eat too much grain or green grass, but a horse'll eat himself sick, and maybe ruin his feet with founderin' if you let him free-feed."

Artie watched Pansy and Pete with new respect.

"Why would anyone want a horse, then, if mules are so much tougher and smarter?" she asked.

"Even a pretty mule is not as good-lookin' as a horse," her dad answered. "Mules ain't really meant for saddle animals, though some folks uses them that way. Horses have a more stylish way of goin', and generally speakin', have more git-up-an-git, though some o' the lighter mules can be pretty fast and high steppin'."

Artie enjoyed the rumble of her father's voice. "Mules are part horse and part donkey, right?" she said.

"Right, though they call 'em jacks, not donkeys." Dad said.

Artie nodded.

"Take Pansy there," Mr. Wilson continued. "She's heavier built than Pete. She's probably out of a draft mare, and he's from a saddle mare. She's a good, steady ol' girl, though. She'll have young Pete workin' real good come fall."

They rode in silence for a while. Then her father said, "I'm thinkin' about gettin' a mule from the stockman, like Grandpa did this one here. Young mule. Green. Want to teach Ballard how to handle a mule afore he gets too old. Always been a mule man in the Wilson line."

Artie grimaced at the picture of her brother fighting a green-broke mule all summer long. He'd hate it. He liked cars, not horses and mules. But she didn't say anything. Instead, she reached back for her green parasol to shade her winter white neck from the sun. The catch was bent, but Artie finally managed to slip it over the latch. The parasol snapped open with a ruffling flop.

As if a rattlesnake had reared up under him, Pete jumped straight up in the air. Pansy shied to the left, jerking Pete off balance as he came back down. He fell into his collar, wrenching the wagon forward and whacking himself and Pansy on the hocks with the wooden bar that connected the mules to the wagon.

That's all it took. With a whiff and a snort they thundered up the hard-packed roadbed, harnesses clanking and the wagon jolting and bumping after them like a tin can on a cat's tail.

Chapter Six

As the mules tore up the road, Artie grabbed for the wagon seat. The offending parasol caught the wind like a sail, jerking her backward. She teetered, dirt whizzing by her in a blur. Scrabbling in desperation, she managed to get a grip on the backrest. One hand still grasped the handle of the green sunshade.

With ears pinned back and big heads stretched out like racehorses, the mules thundered on the hard roadbed, pelting Artie and her dad with bits of gravel, enveloping them in a cloud of dust. Grandpa's old wagon pounded through the chuckholes in the road.

Dad stood, arms straining as he pulled back on

the reins. "Whoa down! Whoa there!" he bellowed, sawing the leather lines back and forth to keep the runaways to the middle of the road. He slashed at the parasol. "Get that durned thing outta sight."

Artie twisted backward and wrestled with the umbrella. The stubborn catch resisted her efforts. Clinging to the board on the back of the seat, she inched her way over and down into the wagon box. Partially sheltered from the wind there, she managed to close the frilly umbrella. About then her father was able to pull the mules down from a dead run into a head-tossing gallop.

The mules fell back to a trot, then a walk as Dad sweet-talked them, and before long the wagon stopped. "Whoa, there, mules," he said in the gentle voice he reserved for animals. The wagon body squeaked as he climbed down.

"Pete, you old jibber," he said, and Artie heard a furry pat. The harness jingled and one of the mules snorted as if disgusted.

Artie shrank lower.

The wagon body tilted and the springs protested once more as her father climbed back aboard. "Giddap," he said, slapping the reins on the mules' backs. The wheels squealed, and they were off again, this time at a slow walk.

The bed of the wagon was hard and Artie felt every bump in the road. She almost wished she'd been thrown out and was lying somewhere behind them. It was comforting to picture herself hurt— but not *too* hurt (bleeding slightly and knocked cold)—sprawled by the side of the road. Her father would run back the way they had come, calling her name, looking, looking. When he saw her, he would tenderly scoop her up in his strong arms and say—

"Artesia May Wilson?" Dad's voice broke in on her dramatic scene. But it was not the sorry, sympathetic voice she had created in her imagination. It held an edge of steel, and Artie knew his eyes would be cold as January.

"Yes?" Artie tried to sound innocent.

"Get up here on this seat. What do you have to say for yourself, girl? Scarin' these mules halfway to next Christmas. It's a thousand wonders an automobile didn't come down the road right about then. We coulda had us some serious injuries, to say nothin' about ruinin' Grandpa's mules and bustin' up his wagon."

Artie took her time climbing up over the seat, glancing sideways at her father's profile. His curls were ruffled from the struggle with the runaway mules, and the blue-black shadow of waiting whiskers gave his tanned face a look of strength.

"Well?" her father demanded, and he glared at her.

"Um—you sure handled those mules well, Dad," Artie said. "You didn't look one bit scared and you knew just what to do." She watched for the effect of her words.

His eyebrows went up, and a dimple appeared in his cheek. Then he poked her in the ribs with his elbow, threw back his head, and laughed. "You do beat all, Artie."

Artie let out a long breath, still shaky from the wild ride.

The rest of the journey was peaceful. The reddish purple of redbud trees and the white dogwood blossoms stood out from the new green of the forest like splotches of paint and white cotton fluff glued on a piece of green paper.

Shortly before 10:00, they passed the general store at Ready and started up Three Mile Hill. Steep and unforgiving, it wound up, up, up into the sky. Finally they topped out and paused to let the mules rest before heading down the other side. This was where Artie's mother always made Dad let out her and the children to walk, weak though she was from TB.

"Reason," Mom would say, "if them brakes don't hold, I'm satisfied we'd all be killed."

Last time, Ballard had stayed on the wagon with Dad, but Mom insisted Artie walk with her. Today, Artie gripped the edge of the seat with excitement made rich with a bit of fear as they started down the far side.

Tall trees lined the way, and their long branches reached out to hold hands over the road, turning it into a tunnel. Here, the yellow sun made dancing shadows on the ground as it shone through the canopy. The mules leaned back against the weight of the wagon. Artie braced her feet on its front edge to keep from sliding out of the seat.

The whole world seemed to be on a slant. Then, peeking around a curve halfway down the hill, Artie could see the white-sided house of her mother's parents. It had been built in 1924, replacing the log cabin in which Mom and Aunt Milly had been born.

The frame house with the big front porch nestled about thirty yards in front of a high, mounded hill, which was pocked with limestone outcroppings, and heavily timbered with oak, hickory, walnut, and elm. Beech trees seemed to march up the ridge.

Artie smiled as she remembered how she and Ballard had gathered the three-cornered beechnuts on their last visit the previous fall. They cracked the fragile shells with their teeth to get to the sweet little meat inside.

Artie loved visiting her grandparents, but the ten miles between them might as well have been a hundred, for as often as they got to make the trip. Sarah Jane and her family could drive all the way to *JOE-ja* if they wanted to. Someday . . . , she told herself.

She could barely sit still as the wagon rolled toward the house. As they stopped with a *whoa* and a jangle of harness, she jumped to the ground to meet Aunt Milly coming out the door.

Milly was tall and merry and full of fun ideas. Artie buried her face in the folds of her blue calico dress, inhaling the mingled scents of sunshine and fresh air with a hint of wood smoke all blended with her special perfume.

Three weeks or more with Aunt Milly! Mom would laugh and be gay, and Dad's fiddle would sing every night to the accompaniment of Aunt Milly's guitar. And as an added bonus for Artie, Aunt Milly could always be counted on to take over Artie's chores while she was at school.

Mammaw stepped outside next and Artie turned to hug her as well. A little wisp of a lady with a thin fluff of snowy hair, Mammaw wore a black print dress that came down to the top of her shoes, with a white apron over it. Artie had never seen her wear any other colors—just black and white. It was as much a part of her grandmother as Mammaw's outlook on life. Things were either right or wrong. There was no middle ground. Artie hugged her hard.

"Good land, Artie, how you've growed. Yer as tall as I am and as strong as a horse," Mammaw said, but the turn of her words let Artie know that being as strong as a horse was a good thing in Mammaw Woosley's book.

Pappaw appeared around the corner of the house just then. His white beard reached to his belt buckle, making him look like Moses' in the Bible, while his sweeping white mustache reminded Artie of an outlaw's. He shook hands with her father and swept Artie into his arms. "How's my Artesia after all these days?"

Pappaw always called her Artesia. Not Artesia May, like Mom or Dad did when she was in trouble. Just Artesia, like she was already a grown lady. She buried her nose in his collar and savored the familiar odors of sweat, lye soap, and tobacco smoke.

They ate a huge dinner of ham—cured in Pappaw's smokehouse—sweet potatoes, and hominy. There was redeye gravy, too, made with coffee and the drippings from the ham. A pone of cornbread filled another platter, accompanied by a choice of blackberry or wild grape jelly. Artie lost count of how many helpings she ate.

At last she pushed her plate away, almost too full

to breathe. Dad and Pappaw tipped their chairs back and sipped black coffee.

"Well, Reason," Pappaw said. "What d'ya think about this here Depression and the stock market crash? D'ya think President Hoover's goin' to pull this country outta hard times purty quick? He keeps a-sayin' that things is turnin' around, but I don't see 'em gettin' better any time soon."

"That Hoover oughta be run out of office, if you ask me," Dad said. "Things has gone from bad to worse since he's been president."

Aunt Milly spoke up. "I think poor old Hoover's just the scapegoat for the way Harding and Coolidge ran the country during the time they were presidents."

Artie's dad picked his teeth with a straw. His eyebrows drew down into a frown. "Why do you say that, Milly?"

Pappaw answered instead. "For years factories been turnin' out so many new things, an' people kept goin' into debt to buy the latest new thing, or to try to make money fast. Had to be only a matter of time till it caught up with 'em."

Artie hoped they wouldn't stay on this subject

too long. Folks talked forever when they got started on politics. Besides, politics had a way of making Dad upset.

"Hoover don't believe in givin' government money to folks to live on," Pappaw continued. "He believes the country's money troubles'll fix themselves if we leave it alone long enough. And besides, he's afeard that if the government starts givin' away money, American families'll lose their independence and determination. They'll just sit back and let someone else feed their children."

Dad leaned back in his chair and nodded. "Sounds like a good idea to me." Artie couldn't tell exactly what part sounded good to him—the government not giving away money or someone else feeding his children.

Apparently Mammaw had had enough of government problems. "How's Katie doin' these days, Reason?"

"Doc says she's doin' fine," Reason said.

"Thought Doc was the one that tol' her she shouldn't be havin' no more young'uns after Artie was born, on account o' the consumption." Mammaw pressed her point.

"Does it make a difference?" Artie watched their faces.

"Not really, Artie," Aunt Milly answered, her smile a little too bright. "Doctors just want their patients to be totally well before they take on as big a project as a new baby."

Artie couldn't help feeling there was more to it than that. But before she could learn more, Pappaw changed the subject. "You still havin' trouble with yer well, Reason?"

"Yeah," Dad said. "Guess the old well is plumb played out. It'd be mighty handy not to have to tote water from the spring."

Not that he ever carries much water himself, Artie thought. The old well hadn't worked for years.

Dad took another swig of coffee. "What I need is a good water witcher."

Water witcher. The name sounded wicked, but Artie was fascinated in spite of herself.

"I'll witch ya a well, Reason," Pappaw said.

"Now, Pappaw," Mammaw protested. "You know I don't like you to call it witchin'. It's dowsin'. Dowsin' for water, or divinin' with a divinin' rod."

"I'll dowse ya a well, then, Reason," Pappaw said with a grin.

"Much obliged, Joshua," Dad said. "But I cain't bring you back fer at least another week. My pa is goin' to be needin' his mules to plow up his corn ground."

"Don't have to go nowhere, Reason," Pappaw said. "I'll dowse it here in my own yard."

"But you're nigh onto ten miles away. Can you do that?" Dad's brows raised in surprise.

"Sure. Cain't think why I hain't done it afore. I'll get me a forked stick and we'll just go dowse it right now." Pappaw gulped the last of the coffee in his cup and pushed away from the table.

Artie pushed her chair back too. "May I be excused?"

"Yes, run along and watch yer pappaw," Mammaw said with a smile. "He be one o' the best dowsers in the country hereabouts. Ye won't see the likes o' his kind very often."

Pappaw selected a forked branch from a tree in the side yard and cut a stick about two feet long. Moving to the porch, he sat down on the step and took the ends of the fork like the top half of a *Y* in either hand, palms up. He turned the stick until it pointed up at a forty-five-degree angle.

"Now, we'll see if you got some water on your place," he said. "Usually you jest walk around till ya feel the stick turnin' in yer hands. The stronger the pull, the closer the water be," Pappaw said.

Artie glanced to see if her father was taking the whole thing seriously. His eyes followed Pappaw's every move.

"Bein' as yer place is ten miles away," said Pappaw, "I'll jest ask this here branch a few questions."

He looked at the stick. "Be there some water on Reason's place?" he asked. The rod dipped. "Be it close to the house?" It dipped again.

"What's it saying?" Artie asked.

Pappaw looked over at her. "When the rod dips toward the ground, it's a-sayin' yes. If it don't move, that means no."

Artie could see his gnarled hands gripping the

stick so hard they turned white at the knuckles, yet the divining rod bobbed and danced like a sapling in a spring wind as he questioned it.

Pappaw looked at Dad. "My rod says ya got some water 'bout a five yards from yer house. Go five paces straight east from yer front door. Drive a stake there. Dig down and you'll find two streams crossed. Should be good water at fifteen feet."

"How do you know, Pappaw?" Artie asked.

"I jest asks my stick. Most dowsers counts the number o' times the rod bobs down'ard over a spot. That'll be how many feet deep," Pappaw said.

"Does the witchin' stick just bob of itself?" Dad asked.

"Yeah. I've had it pull so hard it like to stripped the bark off in my hands. Even had one break right off."

Artie's dad scratched his head. "How can you do this on your place to find water on my place?" he asked.

"Cain't tell ya that, son," Pappaw said. "Jest works, that's all. Not ever'one can do it, but works for me. Here, Artesia. Feel the pull when I asks it questions." Pappaw held one end of the forked stick and offered the other fork to Artie.

As Pappaw questioned it, the rod pulled and jumped in her hand like something alive. Goose-flesh crept up her neck.

"Cain't hardly wait to get back home and start a-diggin'," Reason said, and shook Pappaw's hand. "You're right handy to have in the family."

They went on to talk about guns and dogs, so Artie drifted inside to ask Mammaw if she knew any stories about their ancestors that she could use in her heritage paper. That was all it took to get her grandma in a talking mood.

"Well, if ya go fer enough back, ya got yer great-great-great-grandfather, William Anderson. He done fought in the battle of St. Clair's Defeat. That were in 1791."

"Which war was that, Mammaw?"

"It was one o' them battles that sparked up after the French 'n Injun War, I do believe. An' then there was your great-great-great-*great*-grandpa—he done served with General Washington in Valley Forge. My pappy tol' me that his great-great-grandfather was there when Cornwallis surrendered. Fact is, four of your great-great-great-great-grandpas fought in the Revolutionary War. We been in this country 'bout as long as anyone else. We done shed blood in more than one war. We gived what we could—hard work, honest dealin's, and our lives when necessary."

Warmth welled up within Artie. Somewhere in the dusty past, when the Boston Tea Party was news, her forefathers had been young men not much older than Ballard. They'd sweated and laughed, hoped and loved—yet had been willing to die for this country if need be. The thought brought a lump to Artie's throat. All at once she was gallant, too—brave, ready to sacrifice for the good of—she wasn't sure what, but something worthwhile.

The afternoon whizzed by, and all too soon, Artie's dad and Pappaw had the mules harnessed up and hitched to the wagon. If they didn't leave soon, darkness would catch them before they reached home. Already the afternoon shadows were beginning to stretch out on the ground.

Artie helped Aunt Milly carry her bags and guitar out, and was gratified to see the baskets of food that Mammaw was sending to Mom.

"Tell your mam to rest easy," Mammaw said. "And I'm a-thinkin' of her, and prayin' for the baby to come real easy."

Artie shed a tear or two on Pappaw's rough shoulder.

"There, there, young'un," he soothed. "You'll be back afore you know it." He hoisted her into the wagon.

But Artie knew it would be a long time before she would be there with them again. There was an ache in her chest, deep and lonely, and she waved at the old couple until the wagon rounded a curve and hid them from sight.

Chapter Seven

At school the next week, Artie came to the last page of her fifth-grade reader. Picking up the book with fingers that trembled a bit, she stepped into the aisle and approached Miss Small's desk.

Miss Small looked up. "Do you need something, Artie?"

"Um, I, um—here. I finished this." Artie handed her the book.

Miss Small's face lit up. "Artie, I am proud of you," she whispered with a big smile. "If you keep working this hard, you'll be ready for high school before you know it."

Artie couldn't help grinning as Miss Small stood and rapped on her desk.

"Class, I have an announcement to make."

In front of her fellow students, Artie was suddenly conscious of her mousy hair and faded dress. She could feel the red of embarrassment creeping up and pulsing in her cheeks. Apparently oblivious to Artie's mortification, Miss Small waited until all eyes were staring forward.

"Artie has just completed her fifth-grade reader," Miss Small announced. "She is now ready to be promoted to sixth level." She clapped energetically, as if Artie were a visiting dignitary.

"Artie, you may move your things to the other side of Sarah's desk." Miss Small beamed. "Now, will the first-grade readers come to the front of the room to recite?"

As Artie gathered papers and books from her desk, she whispered goodbye to Eula, then moved to stand beside Sarah Jane's desk. In her daydreams about this moment, Artie planned to feel triumphant, with a little malice mixed in. Instead, she felt unexpectedly apologetic as she watched Sarah Jane's plump hands moving everything off the vacant desk beside her.

Once in her new desk, Artie made a couple of discoveries right away. One, Sarah Jane smelled nice—like soap and clothes dried in the sunshine. Her black curls were silky and smooth. Probably washes her hair twice a week, Artie thought. I guess I could, too, she added. No one said I couldn't bathe midweek, even though it meant an extra time of hauling and heating water. If Dad ever got around to digging the new well, I wouldn't have to haul the water so far. Maybe I could even rinse out my school dress in the middle of the week so it didn't smell so—well, so used—by Friday. Of course, that would mean another time of ironing with irons heated on the woodstove.

Discovery number two: Sarah Jane was left-handed. All day, Artie and Sarah Jane bumped elbows when they wrote. At first Artie tried to ignore it, but soon it became annoying. Sarah Jane seemed to think Artie bumped her on purpose. But when Artie suggested they switch chairs to solve the problem,

Sarah Jane acted like Artie had offered to spit on the Holy Bible. After that, Artie took a wicked pleasure in every encounter.

Later in the day Miss Small stepped outside. Artie was working on her contest paper when Sarah Jane's elbow again bumped hers, crippling the leg on her capital *M*. She jabbed back.

Sarah Jane gave a small, ladylike snort, but didn't move her arm.

"Get your elbow out of my way," Artie whispered. "You're crowding onto my side." She glared at her new seatmate.

"I was here first," Sarah Jane said, in a condescending voice. "I—"

Miss Small stepped back inside before Sarah Jane could finish her sentence. Artie lifted one corner of her lip in a smirk, then took her pencil and drew a dark line straight down the middle of the desktop.

Yet the rest of that day, the pencil barrier bothered her. The more she thought about it, the more she wished she hadn't drawn that dividing line between them.

When she got home, Artie planned to go digging

roots like she'd told Mom she would, but with Aunt Milly there, it was hard to make herself leave the house. Mom and Aunt Milly giggled and talked like two schoolgirls while they worked on the dress Artie would wear for May Meeting, and Artie wanted to be in on the fun.

The prospect of May Meeting brought a wealth of pictures and stories to Artie's mind. Great-Grandfather John Wilson had pioneered a church over in the Welch's Creek area of Butler County, and built a building to worship in. A few years later, though, the congregation had a falling-out, and Great-Grandfather Wilson decided to build a new church. Dad liked to tell the story.

"Ol' John figgered the ones that kept to the old church just might burn his new church, so he done built his new church right upside the old one, barely thirty foot away. That way if they tried to burn his church, they'd burn theirs too." And there the churches still stood, side by side.

Shortly after that time, Artie's great-grandfather began the tradition of May Meeting. It was like a huge family reunion held on the second Sunday of

May each year. There would be singing, preaching, and dinner on the grounds.

John Wilson passed away, but family members continued the custom of May Meeting. For the last three years, Mom's health had prevented them from making the twenty-five-mile trip to the Wilson Home Church. Then last month Dad had announced, "Katie, I'm goin' to May Meeting this year to see my kinfolk."

"But, Reason," Mom had said, "the baby's almost due; I'm not sure I can make that trip. What if it comes when you're gone?"

"You can go or stay, but I'm not goin' to miss another May Meeting."

Mom had seemed to shrink three inches when Dad said that. Artie wanted to say to him, "Isn't it your baby too?"

But now Aunt Milly was here. She would stay until after the baby was born. With the prospect of her company, Mom seemed to feel much better about letting Dad go to May Meeting without her.

That evening Aunt Milly added bright pink flowers to Artie's old straw hat, and Artie's dress took shape under Mom's skillful needle. Green like the new leaves of spring, the fabric had little yellow and pink flowers dancing across it. The dress had a dropped waist, pleated skirt, and V neck, and would have a white collar with a big green bow. Artie was sure she'd seen the exact style in the Sears and Roebuck catalog. Mom must have looked at the picture and created the pattern out of newspaper.

At school the next day, Artie erased the pencil line on the desk before Sarah Jane arrived. When Miss Small dictated spelling words, Sarah Jane again jostled Artie's elbow, but before Artie could snort or retort, Sarah Jane said, "Excuse me."

Artie had been primed to hold on to every inch that belonged to her even though she had erased the dividing line, but Sarah Jane's apology disarmed her. There had been tension between them ever since Sarah Jane started coming to Buck Creek two years before. In all that time, Artie couldn't remember Sarah Jane saying one nice thing to her. And now here she was apologizing.

With Aunt Milly waiting at home, Artie had no desire to linger after school. The week sped by and it was Friday afternoon before she knew it. At the cross-roads, where the group of mailboxes huddled together like sheep, Ballard checked the Wilson mailbox.

"Hey, look, Art. Here's a letter for Aunt Milly." He turned it over. "Looks like it's from Mammaw."

"Wonder why she'd be writin', using all that money on a stamp?" Artie said. "Aunt Milly hasn't been gone very long."

Ballard shrugged and stowed the letter in his pocket. "Guess we'll find out."

When they reached home, Mom and Aunt Milly were sipping tea in Mom's bedroom. Ballard handed the letter to their aunt.

Something about the way Aunt Milly puckered her lips as she read it prepared Artie for bad news.

"Well, Katie, I'm mighty sorry to say this, but it looks like Ma needs me at home. Pa has sprained his ankle pretty bad, and she's been trying to do all the chores by herself."

Mom nodded, but her hand shook a little as she set her teacup down.

"You could come home with me," Aunt Milly said. "Then I could help you when the baby comes."

A light rose in Mom's blue eyes, then faded behind a film of tears. "No. Reason don't like me to be gone. 'Sides, if I go, there won't be no one to care for Artie and Ballard."

"Aw, Mom," Ballard said. "Art and me would be just fine. We could take care of the place and I'd watch over Artie real good."

"Please say yes, Mom," Artie begged. "It would only be for a few weeks. We'd be just fine. I'd cook for Dad." She didn't add that she did most of the cooking as it was.

Aunt Milly doubled her efforts at persuasion as well, but Mom was unmoved. She would stay home and go to May Meeting with Dad, and everything would work out just fine.

Artie hoped she was right.

A neighbor came the next morning to take Aunt Milly home. Her going left such a hole that life seemed gray and drained of energy. It didn't help that rain moved in over the area and turned everything into a sea of mud.

Artie hated rain. She hated how they had to set pans and buckets around the house to catch the water that dripped through the roof. It soaked through the pages from the Sears and Roebuck catalog Mom had pasted on the ceiling to keep the drafts out, and it seeped in under the front door.

Besides, Mom wouldn't let Artie and Ballard go to school in this much rain. By the time they arrived at Buck Creek, their shoes would be wet through and caked with mud, and their clothes damp all day. Artie hated missing school, getting behind in her books.

So they were shut in at home, surrounded by the plopping of raindrops in various corners of the house. Artie tried to work on her essay. For some reason, getting her thoughts down on paper was like trying to capture and hold the water that bubbled out of the spring and tumbled over the creek bed and away. She wasn't just competing against Sarah Jane, but the students in the nearby schools as well, and Artie couldn't seem to get past the first page.

But if she didn't win that twenty-five-dollar savings bond, how would she ever make it to high school? Ten pounds of mayapple roots sold for fifty cents. Due to rain, and Aunt Milly's visit, she'd only been able to dig about four pounds so far. After they dried out enough not to mold, that would be approximately two pounds' worth. Ten cents. If one cent out of every five went toward her high school fund, that would come to the grand total of two cents.

All that week Artie labored on her essay, and by the time school ended on Friday, she'd reached the final few paragraphs.

The next week, the Saturday before May Meeting, Grandma came down, and she and Artie cooked all sorts of food to take with them, while Mom sat nearby to visit.

It's a good thing Mammaw sent so many goodies, Artie thought as she tucked a jar of beet pickles into a basket, or else all we'd have to bring from our house would be leftover coon and corn pone.

As it was, the bulk of what they prepared came from Grandma's pantry. Smoked Kentucky ham, boiled eggs, cucumber pickles, custard pies and wheat biscuits—it was all Artie could do not to snitch bites all day long.

"Katie," Artie overheard Grandma saying that afternoon. "I'm concerned that the wagon ride'll be too much for you. Don't want that baby a-comin' afore its time. You still got a good two weeks to go."

"Now don't go to frettin', Grandma," Mom said. "I'm goin' to take a pillow, and that spring wagon of yers rides real nice."

Grandma persisted. "Why don't you stay home? I know you want Reason to be there when the baby comes, but he'd be comin' home the same night anyway."

But Mom shook her head.

The second Sunday in May—May 11, 1930— dawned damp and overcast. Dad brought Pansy and Pete down, and they stood harnessed, hitched to the wagon, and ready to go. Artie and Ballard carried out the food baskets and stowed them safely in the wagon box, covering them with cloths.

Dad helped Mom up to the high seat, the baby within her spreading her skirt like a one-sided hoop. Tucking a lap robe around her, he tickled her under the chin. "You're lookin' real chipper this morning, Katie, just like the first time we went to May Meeting together back in our courtin' days."

But her mother already looked white and tired.

Inside the wagon box there was a mound of hay to feed the mules. Ballard spread a blanket over it and he and Artie sat down. Then with a clink and a jangle, Pete and Pansy stepped out. Artie hoped Pete would behave today. Mom might not have the strength to hold on if he took off running.

For the first ten of the twenty-five miles, the mules moved in a steady trot, and the air was full of early morning smells. Then the drizzle began. Artie's perky straw hat with the pink flowers began to give off the sweet smell of wet straw, and now and then a trickle of water ran down the back of her neck. She and Ballard pulled the blanket over their shoulders in an effort to keep dry.

The road got muddier and muddier. Soon the mules slowed to a walk. Their feet made sucking noises as they plodded along, and the wheels tossed up chunks of mud as high as the sides of the wagon. Artie scooched closer to Ballard in the center of the wagon, hoping to escape the blops that occasionally flung over. It was cold, drizzly, and not at all how Artie had dreamed the trip to May Meeting would be. Boring, too. At last she could stand the monotony no longer. She stood, braving the rain to hang over the seat and hear the grown-ups talk.

But as soon as she stuck her head between them, they quit talking. When she pulled back, her hat stuck under Dad's elbow and a little breeze sent it tumbling into the road. Then there was a crunch.

"Stop, stop! My hat! You ran over my hat!" she shrieked, and pulled at Dad's arm.

As Dad reined the mules to a halt, Artie stumbled over Ballard to the back of the wagon. There in the road behind them lay her pretty little hat, smashed and muddy.

"Oh, Mom, it's ruined," Artie wailed. She started to climb down to rescue the hat.

"No, no, Artie," Mom said. "Just leave it be. It's too muddy to wear now. You'll get your shoes all messed up besides. You'll just have to go without a hat."

Without a hat? "But Mom," Artie whined. "All the other ladies and girls will have hats on. I'll be the only one. *Nobody* goes to May Meeting without a hat."

"I know," Mom said. "But there's no help for it now. You'll just have to go the way you are."

Artie pouted and sniffled the rest of the endless way to May Meeting. During the last half hour or so, the drizzle stopped. Artie decided she'd better dry up too, so no one would know she'd been crying. It was going to be bad enough to be without a hat, never mind having red eyes too.

Dad pulled up to the picnic grounds. Colorful clothes covered the ground like earthbound flags. Folks from all over rattled up in buggies, in wagons, or on horseback. Boys darted in and out among groups of people, playing tag. Women arranged their dishes and directed their children, while off to one side, men tethered their teams and swapped the news of the day.

Artie tingled. She had been only nine the last time she'd come to May Meeting. She jumped out of the wagon and waited while Ballard helped Mom down from the seat.

Their mother smoothed her dark blue dress, then reached up to unpin her hat and set it on Artie's head. "There. That looks nice. Good thing we done trimmed it in pink. Matches your dress just fine."

"Mom! I can't wear your hat."

"Why not?" Mom calmly inserted a hat pin to hold the hat to Artie's head.

Artie read determination in her mother's eyes. But Artie was determined too. "No, Mom," she said, and reached up to unpin the hat. "I shouldn't have thrown such a fit when I lost mine. It's better for a girl to be hatless than a grown woman, especially one that's going to have a baby." She placed the hat back on her mother's head and handed her the pin. "Thank you, though. I'll be fine. You know I hate hats anyway."

Mom gave Artie a tight squeeze. Pressed against her mother's round belly, Artie felt the baby kick out beneath her.

Together Mom, Artie, and Ballard unloaded the food from the wagon. Artie felt a new fellowship with her mother, as if they were partners, not just parent and child. She wondered if it would be that way when she was grown up—two women together, sharing difficulties, dreams, and duties. She hoped so.

Chapter Eight

By late morning, most folks had arrived at May Meeting. As the rain moved out of the area, a warm sun beamed down, making the ground steam and drying out damp travelers. Artie decided that she would just pretend she had a hat on like everyone else. Wandering in and out among the groups of people, she looked for cousins and friends. Dad had gone to take care of the mules, and she could see Ballard talking with a bunch of boys over by the fence.

"Hey, Artie! Over here!" Artie located the owner of the voice—her second cousin Zilda Daniels, ten years old. And beside Zilda stood her big sister, Zethy.

Of all people to see me without a hat, Artie thought with a groan. Zethy was thirteen—tall and willowy, with blonde hair that swept over one eye and was covered with a cloche, a hat a movie star would wear.

Artie tossed her short brown hair and smoothed her rain-rumpled dress as she approached the girls. "Hi, Zilda. Hi, Zethy."

Zethy swept her eyes over Artie. When she reached Artie's hatless head, she sucked in her cheeks and tilted her head. "No hat, Artie?" she drawled.

Artie's cheeks burned. What business was it of Zetha Daniels' if Artie wore a hat or not? She tossed her hair again and said, "Latest fashion, Zethy."

Zethy's sleek brows came down momentarily. "I prefer to be called Zetha, not Zethy, and I'm not aware of any such new *style.*"

Artie couldn't think of anything to say. Zilda came to her rescue. Grabbing her by her arm, she pulled Artie toward a group of girls, leaving Zetha posed like a languishing model.

On the way, Zilda asked, "Hey, Artie. Is it really a new fashion?"

Artie grinned weakly. "No," she said. "Lost mine under the wagon wheel on the way here."

"Do you want I should run over home and get you one of mine? I got one with pink flowers on it." Zilda and Zetha lived just down the road from the church. John Wilson had been their great-grandfather as well as Artie's.

"A hat would be great, Zilda," Artie said. "If you don't mind."

The girl ran down the road. Before too long she panted up to Artie with a straw sailor hat in her outstretched hand. "Here," she gasped. "Took me a couple minutes to find it."

Artie felt herself go pale. It was a little girl's hat. Compared to Zetha's stylish cloche, going hatless would be better than appearing in this. But then she'd hurt Zilda's feelings. Artie took the hat with its pink blossoms and tried to smile at Zilda as she settled the straw creation on her head. It perched up there like a teacup.

"I guess it's too little for me, Zildy," Artie said with a sigh. She hoped Zilda wouldn't realize it was a sigh of relief. "But thank you anyway. It was right nice of you to share with me. Do you mind if I don't wear it?"

Zilda looked disappointed, but said, "No, that's all right." She took the hat and trudged back down the road.

Artie wandered over to another group of cousins. They giggled and talked of school, friends, the Depression, and clothes until the preacher took his place. Then silence fell. Thomas Kelly was a huge man—six foot four inches, someone said, and nigh unto three hundred pounds. One of the cousins whispered, "My dad said Brother Kelly comes from Arkansas. Got in a fight with a man there over somethin' in the Bible and landed them both in jail. He's a real ringtail roarer, Brother Kelly is."

Artie thought he looked like one, for sure. His hair was fiery red, his skin reddish too, and gray-green Irish eyes blazed out at the seated people. But he also had a huge grin that made her feel at home.

Artie looked around her at the people sitting on their various blankets, like so many bunches of multi-colored flowers on the bright grass of spring. A bittersweet feeling washed over her. Funny, she thought.

We've gathered from all over the place to join here. Tonight we'll all go home, and maybe not see each other ever again. But for now, for May Meeting, we are joined.

Mr. Kelly's voice rumbled like thunder. "My text for today is Isaiah"—he said it *eye-ZIE-uh*—"Can the clay say to the Potter, 'What are you making?'

"People ask, 'Why did God make me poor and So-and-So rich?'" he said.

"They say, 'God, you're not fair. Do you love them more than me?'"

Thomas Kelly strode back and forth across the grassy speaking area. "Let me ask you, people—can clay form itself into a vessel?"

There was a spattering of noes in answer.

"Does the clay know what kind of a vessel the Potter wants to make?"

"No."

"Does the clay know what tools the Potter should use?"

"No." Each time, the response was louder and stronger.

"Then I asks you"—Brother Kelly towered over

the crowd like a judge delivering a verdict—"can the clay say to the Potter, 'Why have you made me thus?'" His voice rose to a feverish pitch and he slammed his huge fist down on the speaker's stand.

An enthusiastic chorus of noes and amens followed. Artie liked the way people got to take part in the meeting. Sometimes it got really wild—whoops and whistles and waving arms. She'd even seen one brush arbor meeting where folks ran down the aisles crying, and she'd heard of others where people rolled on the floor and spoke in strange languages like the Bible talked about on the day of Pentecost.

Mr. Kelly preached on. He told some stories. He made people laugh. He made them cry. But as he talked on and on, drowsiness tugged on Artie's eyelids and hunger pinched at her belly. She wished she dared drift over to where the food waited and snatch a few cookies. Stretching her legs out in front of her, she stifled a yawn.

"Brothers and sisters—have you ever considered that your heavenly Father has a special plan for each of you?" Brother Kelly paused, sweat dripping from his red face.

If God had a plan for her, Artie sure hoped it was the same as her own plan.

"If God wanted us to be the same, He'd a made us the same," he said, pausing dramatically. "What if all you had in your house was buckets? Buckets to eat out of and buckets to cook in and buckets to sit on? If you needed to fetch water or milk a cow, you'd need a good bucket. But if you wanted to comb your hair, a bucket ain't goin' to work too well."

Artie laughed along with the others.

Mr. Kelly roared on, waving his arms with great sweeping gestures. "That's the way it is with God," he said. "We have different kinds of work on the earth, and so He forms us through different kinds of circumstances and gives us different gifts so we will be able to do what He prepares us for.

"So the next time you ask God why He has made you male or female, rich or poor, sick or well, just remember, as it says in the Good Book—He knows how to form clay into vessels 'fit for the Master's use.'"

Brother Thomas Kelly mopped his forehead and stepped back from the speaking area to a chorus of amens. With that, the morning preaching session ended.

Everyone stood, stretched, and headed for the spread of good things to eat. "Come on, Artie," Zilda said. "Let's go get some food."

After the noon meal came the second preaching session. Another man, as small and dark as Brother Kelly was large and red, talked on and on about Job and Moses and Abraham, and Artie felt like curling up somewhere for a nap.

It was hard being too old for some things and too young for others. A grown-up could get up and wander by the food, pick up a biscuit or a piece of ham, and pour a cup of coffee for herself. Little kids could curl up with their heads on their dad's shoulder or mom's lap and snooze a boring sermon away. But big girls like Artie just had to endure. She looked around for Ballard. He was probably off with a bunch of boys doing fun things like exploring or grooming horses.

Gazing over the crowd, Mom's dark blue dress and pink-trimmed straw hat caught Artie's eye. Mom looked tired. Really tired. She didn't look strong enough to survive the ride home, much less a birth. Artie shivered. Suddenly sleep was not a problem. She got up, regardless of the sermon, and made her way to her mother's side.

"Mom," she whispered. "You all right?"

Mom smiled, but it didn't touch her eyes. "Just tired, Artie. It's uncomfortable sittin' so long."

"Can I get you something?" Artie asked.

"Maybe a drink of that pink lemonade I had earlier," Mom said. "That tasted right nice."

Artie took her mother's mug and walked importantly over to the big jug of lemonade. She snitched a nibble of cake as she stood there, and would have liked to have grabbed a handful of cookies too, but they were just out of reach, and she didn't want to draw attention to herself. As it was, she dropped the ladle when she went to dip the lemonade, and it made a frightful clang.

"Thank you, Artie," Mom said, when she returned. "This tastes wonderful."

"Can I do anything else for you, Mom?"

Her mom was silent for more than a minute. Artie thought perhaps she hadn't heard the question, and was about to repeat it, when her mom replied, "Could you let your father know that I need to go? Now?"

Did Artie hear her right? Mom would never dream of interrupting Dad when he was with the men. Especially at May Meeting. She peered under the shadow of Mom's hat, hoping Mom's eyes would tell her something different. But they were closed. Mom's thin hand crept up to cover the baby within her. Artie picked up her mother's fan and fanned her pale face as she searched for her father's figure in the sea of people.

There. Over by the mules. Good.

"There's Dad," Artie said, "I'll be right back."

Artie worked her way toward the fence where the teams were tied. Her dad stood in the knot of men who leaned against one of the wagons there. As usual, his laughter and stories had the men hanging on his every word.

Artie stepped up to the group. Moments dragged by as she waited for her father to notice her. When he did, he took his time before asking what she needed.

Motioning him down, Artie whispered in his ear,

"Mom says she needs to go. Now. She sent me to see if you're ready."

Anger crossed his face, iced his lake blue eyes, and hid his dimples. The smile was back in a blink, but the eyes stayed cold and half closed.

Artie felt her own eyes narrow. If he got mad and stubborn right then she'd just find Ballard and take Mom home herself.

"Well, guess the wife's gotta go," Dad said. "See you boys later. Mike, I'll get in touch with you about that mule. You come by my gun shop and see if there's somethin' there you'd like to trade for him." He shook hands all around, and turned to tighten Pansy and Pete's harnesses and put their bridles back on.

Artie hurried to find Ballard and to gather their baskets and some food for the homeward journey. It was early afternoon by the time they left. Mom lay on the hay in the back of the wagon, eyes closed, seeming to hardly breathe.

Dad barely said three words the whole way home. The muddy roads kept the mules at a walk, and after what seemed days later, they pulled into the Wilson yard at about seven o'clock that evening.

Ballard helped Artie get their mom down from the wagon, and then began to unload the baskets. Reason Wilson sat statue-still on the seat, staring off into the gloom of the surrounding woods. Artie supported her mother up the porch, into the shadowy house, and onto her bed, where she lay without moving.

Artie lit the kerosene lamp, hoping to brighten the situation. "There, Mom. Do you want to undress now?"

"No. Just need to rest." Her mother's eyes closed again, her bony face drawn and white.

Artie tried to keep her hands from shaking as she removed her mother's shoes and pulled the patchwork quilt up. Something was terribly wrong. Her mother never allowed anyone to *sit* on the beds, much less go to bed with their clothes on.

"I-I-I'll make you some tea." Artie fled to the kitchen. She kindled a fire in the cookstove with trembling fingers. The only prayer she could muster up was "Oh-please-oh-please-oh-please," while she waited for the kettle to boil.

When she took the steaming tea into the bedroom, her mother opened her eyes. "Artie, would ya have Ballard come here, please?"

Artie ran to the barn to get her brother. In the corral behind, she found him brushing mud from Pansy's legs and belly. "Bal, she's asking for you," Artie told him, her fingernails gripping his arm.

Ballard said nothing, but laid the brush on top of a post, vaulted over the rail, and sprinted toward the house. As Artie came in the front door, he emerged from the bedroom. He seemed to have aged years in those few moments.

"She asked me to fetch Doc Miller. Baby's comin'."

Tonight? Artie's stomach churned. "It's not time."

"I know." Ballard lit the railroad lantern that hung by the door, crammed his cap over his rough brown hair, and strode out into the coming twilight.

A small moan from the bedroom set Artie's heart pounding. Should she be doing something in there? What if the baby needed to be born before Doc Miller arrived? Artie had no idea how to deliver a baby.

Where was Dad? Artie went to the porch. "Dad? Dad?" she called, listening for an answer, but none came.

There was another moan from the bedroom. Artie tiptoed into the small room and touched her mother on the shoulder. "Mom, do you want I should go fetch Grandma?"

"No, don't leave me alone, honey," Mom said, and fumbled for Artie's hand. "Doc will be here soon."

Artie stood for a while just holding the thin hand. Mom lay very still, eyes closed. She might have been asleep except for the intervals when she seemed to tense up, breathe deeply, and give a little moaning sigh at the end.

Drifting over to the open door, Artie stared out into the night, willing Ballard and the doctor to arrive in time.

Chapter Nine

Mom's moans started coming closer together and louder. Artie bit her lip. It had been a mistake not to go after Grandma, regardless of her mom's wishes. It would have taken only fifteen, maybe twenty minutes—but now there was even less time. A tear slipped out and trickled down her cheek as she stirred the fire in the cookstove and filled the kettle with more water.

Then she heard footsteps. Artie charged into the living room. Grandma opened her arms and Artie found refuge in her ample embrace.

"Ballard stopped by and left a note on his way to fetch the doctor, but I was up to the neighbor's, else

I'd a been here sooner," she said. "How's she doin', Artie?"

"Don't know. She's moanin' closer together and louder."

Grandma released Artie and started for the kitchen, rolling her sleeves as she went. Artie followed.

"Doc should be here purty soon, iffen he's a-comin'. I'll just wash my hands and get ready."

About that time Dad drifted in the door and started rummaging through the food baskets on the table.

"Reason." Grandma's voice cut like steel. "Your wife needs you. Wash those hands of yours and git in there."

Artie shrank against the doorway as Dad's brows came down and his jaw jutted out.

"Go." Grandma spoke to her son as if he were a small child.

Dad glared at Grandma. But without a word, he washed his hands and stalked into the parlor bedroom where Mom lay.

Before Grandma went into Mom's room, she set

Artie to fetching firewood and boiling water. Artie was glad to have something—anything—to do. She put a big pot of water on to heat, then laid in enough wood to last two days before she quit. As she stacked the last few chunks, she heard the jingling of harness and pounding of horse's hooves flying down the long driveway.

Mom cried out, louder than before. Artie's legs felt as weak as skimmed milk as she went to the porch to watch the buggy flash across the little creek. A bright moon lit the way as it pulled up to the porch steps. Doc Miller handed Ballard the reins and climbed out, bringing his black bag with him.

Ballard motioned Artie over. "How's Mom?"

"No baby yet, Bal. You made it in time. Dad and Grandma got here a few minutes ago."

Ballard nodded. "Met Dad on the way to town. Hoped he'd head back home." He clucked to the doctor's horse and set off for the barn.

Artie plodded up the steps and into the living room where her bed and Ballard's lined the walls. Minutes dragged by, each seeming hours long.

When Ballard came in from tending to the horse, he came close and whispered, "Everything all right?"

To Artie's dismay, tears spouted from her eyes. Ballard drew her into the circle of his arms and patted her on the back. She managed to stop crying and sniffed back the remaining tears. Ballard released her.

"I don't know, Bal." Artie tried hard to sound brave. "She's crying out pretty often. I wonder if that means it's real close."

As the cries from the bedroom grew wilder, Dad came out. His face looked pale under his whisker shadow. He slumped into a chair.

"Fetch me a cup of coffee, will you, Artie-gal?" he said.

Glad for something to do, Artie leaped to comply. As she waited for the water to drip down through the coffee grounds, a terrible moaning cry pierced the air.

Then all was silent, as if the whole house held its breath. She reached for the coffeepot. Just then a thin wail like a bleating lamb sliced the quiet. Artie dropped the cup she was holding and raced into the living room.

Another wail. The baby!

The three of them waited until Artie could stand it no longer. Tiptoeing to the doorway, she opened the door and peeked in. Grandma beamed at her from across the room and held up a tiny, red-faced bundle, swaddled to its ears with a snowy blanket.

"You got a new brother, Artie," Grandma said.

Artie hardly gave the baby a glance. Doc Miller was still bent over the bed. Artie edged close to the head to get a look at her mother, who lay like a wisp on the threadbare pillow. In the yellow lamplight, the shadows under her eyes looked like bruises. But when she saw Artie, she smiled and held out a hand.

Artie gripped it like a drowning man grips a life preserver. "You okay, Mom?" she asked. What she really wanted to say was, "Are you going to live?"

"I'm fine, Artie-girl." Her voice sounded weak, but happy, and Artie breathed a little easier. "Baby's here, and he's just fine too. Do you want to hold him?"

Artie didn't, but she said, "Sure," and took the little bundle from her grandma.

"Hold his head now, so it don't fall back,"

Grandma said. "Babies ain't strong enough to hold their heads up right at first."

Artie didn't know what to do with her suddenly awkward elbows and hands. She'd never held a newborn before. His tiny face was as red as if he'd been sunburned, and there was a purplish mark above one eye. Dark, wispy hair straggled across a soft head, and he had no eyebrows or eyelashes. She couldn't tell the color of his eyes, as they were closed. He wasn't very pretty, but as she held him there, his little body felt trusting and warm in her arms. She gathered him more securely against her.

Doc Miller worked over Mom for what seemed forever. Artie stayed, watching Mom's breathing, listening for coughing or other danger signals. The baby slept in her arms.

At last the doctor seemed satisfied. He buckled his black bag and went into the other room. "You got yourself another fine son, Reason," Artie heard him say. "Yep, he's going to be just fine."

Artie heard the door open and shut and figured Ballard must be going to harness up Doc's horse. Then the doctor's voice dropped to a rumble, and

Artie couldn't make out what he was saying. She handed the baby to Grandma and went out into the kitchen to listen.

But Doc Miller stopped when he saw her. "Well, Artesia," he said, "how do you like your new brother?"

"Oh, fine," she answered. "Can I get you some coffee or something to eat, Doctor Miller?"

"A cup of coffee would be nice," he said, patting her on the head. "But nothing to eat. I'd better be getting on home. The missus'll be looking for me."

The doctor sipped his coffee and visited with Dad. Then after checking on Mom a final time, he picked up his bag and turned to go.

"Reason, I'll peek in on Katie tomorrow. If you need anything before then, don't hesitate to come get me."

Turning to Artie, he said, "Artesia, why don't you walk out with me to see if Ballard has brought my horse and buggy around."

The doctor's black mare stood in the yard, a darker shadow than the night around her. Ballard finished checking the collar and turned to join them. As the man climbed into his buggy he said, "Children, your mother is very weak. She really shouldn't have had another child. But she did, and pulled through better than I expected her to. She's not out of the woods yet, though, and she's going to need a lot of help. Can I count on you two to take care of her and make sure she doesn't overdo?"

Artie swallowed. "Sure," she managed to croak. Ballard nodded.

Doc Miller gathered up the reins. "Thanks, kids. Now remember what I said. And one other thing: Make sure your mother eats well, or she'll not have any milk for the baby." He snapped the reins on the back of the trim little mare, and the buggy spun in a circle and rattled out of the yard.

Artie looked up at Ballard and saw her own feelings reflected on his tired face.

"Artie," he said. "We got to—" His voice broke, and he blinked rapidly.

Artie's own eyes filled. "We will," she whispered, feeling for his hand. "We will."

Grandma Wilson stayed the rest of the night, and Artie woke Monday morning to the smell of breakfast cooking. Before Grandma went home, she left full instructions for Artie and Ballard. Dad shaved and went on to Caneyville to open his gun shop. And the baby slept, snuggled next to Mom with her arm around him.

"Have you named him yet, Mom?" Artie asked.

Mom smiled. "Simon. Simon John. Ain't he so perfect, Artie?"

Artie and Ballard stayed home from school again the next day to help out. Doc stopped by and said Mom was doing fine. Grandma bustled down the hill bringing some squirrel stew and words of instruction.

"Now you be sure an' fetch me if you need anything," she said, patting Ballard on the shoulder.

"Sure, Grandma," he said.

But somehow no one thought about calling Grandma when little Simon John began to cry. It seemed he cried all day long. Mom was too weak to do much with him, so Artie and Ballard took turns walking up and down, bouncing the wailing baby, who seemed to grow weaker with each passing hour.

The next morning, Artie's dad slapped his hand

down on the table so hard the cups rattled. "How's a man supposed to get a decent night's sleep with that bawlin' goin' on all the time? Cain't even sleep in my own bed." He glared at Artie as if it were all her fault. "You find some way to shut that kid up or I'm sleepin' in town." He stalked out the door and slammed it behind him.

Artie looked at Ballard, who was bouncing Simon in a gentle, constant sway. His eyes glittered, and for the second time in a week, she saw him blinking to hold back tears. From where Artie stood, she could see Mom's stricken face, as if someone had just slapped her. Picking up the bowl of soup that she had just dished out, Artie went into the bedroom.

"Here, Mom, you've got to eat something. Get strong again."

As if she'd been strong before.

"No thank you, Artie. Don't feel like eatin' right now," Mom said, and closed her eyes. "Not hungry."

Artie set the soup on the dresser. From the kitchen, she could hear Ballard's droning, "Shhh, shhh, shhh," and Simon's fragile wail. The constant noise pressed on her ears, and she understood why her father had slammed out the door, grown man though he was.

"Mom?"

"Yes?" Mom's eyes stayed closed.

"Why did you have the baby?" Once the words started, Artie couldn't keep them back. "We were better off before. All he does is cry all the time. You're sick and could even have died."

She fell down with her face in Mom's blanket and exploded. All the tears she'd bottled up the past weeks and months poured out in heaves and sobs. She cried and hiccupped and cried some more. She felt her mother's fingers in her hair, gentle as an evening breeze, lifting, cooling. The tears subsided, but Artie's words stood black and ugly in the air between them.

There was silence for a long time, except for the continued mewling cries from out in the kitchen and Ballard's patient, "Shhh, Simon, shhh, baby." Artie lifted her head and wiped her eyes.

At last Mom spoke. "Not better off, Artie. Not better off, just easier."

Artie sniffed her drippy nose.

"Artie-girl, you know that someday I will die, don't you? Maybe not now, but someday?"

Artie nodded.

Her mother's quiet voice continued. "One of the real special things about having children, besides giving life to another human being, is that there is a little bit of you in that child. Think about this, Artie—if I didn't have no children, then when I died, I'd be gone. But in each of you children is a little bit of me. So in a way, though I might be dead, part of me is gonna live on."

Artie stood up. "I'm sorry, Mom, that I busted out that way."

"Sometimes a body's got to speak out what's inside so it don't eat 'em up," Mom said. "But think about what I've said."

Artie flashed a watery smile. "Could you eat some soup now, Mom? You really should, you know. Help you get well." She helped raise her mother to a sitting position and handed her the bowl of soup.

Back in the kitchen, Artie ladled soup for Ballard and herself. As she gazed into her bowlful, the doctor's words came back to her—*Make sure your mother eats well, or she'll not have any milk for the baby.*

Artie stared at little Simon, cradled in Ballard's arms. The baby had lost the round, full look he had had on the day he was born. He was thin. Thin like a little old man. His cheeks sunk in like Mom's. His crying was almost a moan. Ballard stared at the opposite wall, his own face old and tired.

"Ballard, I'm going to Grandma's," Artie said. "I'll be back soon." Without waiting for his answer, she ran out the door and headed up the hill to their grandparents' farm.

"Grandma! Grandma!" she gasped as she reached the porch.

"In here, child. Somethin' wrong?" Grandma looked startled.

"No, no. I mean yes, but—" Artie paused to get her breath back. Her lungs and legs burned.

"Yer ma?"

"No, it's the baby. He's crying all the time," Artie said.

"Land sakes alive, child. Why didn't you tell me afore this?"

"I thought all babies cried. But now I'm thinking that he's starving," Artie said. "Can we make one of those sugar teats for Simon John like you made for me when I was born? Or is there something else we could feed him?"

"Course the poor thing is hungry. Yer ma is so weak she don't have enough milk to keep a mouse alive right now. I shoulda thought of that afore." She rummaged in the kitchen cabinet and turned around with a can in her hand. "Here. Yer aunt over to Caneyville give me this here evaporated milk last Christmas. You take it back home, pour a little water in to thin it down, and feed that little babe. I'll be down a bit later to check on him, soon's I can get this cornbread off the fire."

Artie charged back downhill, the metal of the precious can gripped hard against her side. Once in the kitchen, she pierced the top in two places and poured about a half inch of the yellowish milk into a cup. Taking hot water from the stove, she put in enough to make a half a cup, mixed it thoroughly, and touched a spoonful of the mixture to her lips to test the temperature. Then, without a word, she lifted the tiny bundle of baby from her brother's arms and sat down.

Taking just a few drops in the spoon, Artie tipped it into the wailing mouth. The baby gave a startled look, opening his eyes wide, and his tiny tongue showed for a moment.

Artie fed him a few more drops. Yes. He was definitely swallowing. And not crying. The silence was suddenly loud. He made sucking noises as the milk went in. Some dribbled down his miniature chin, and his excited jerks caused her to spill once in a while.

The cup was nearly empty when, at last, the little eyes closed and Simon John gave a small sigh of contentment. Artie held him up to her cheek and felt the petal softness of his baby skin, cool against her hot face. He smelled like flowers and milk, and he lay so trustingly in her arms. She swayed back and forth, and from deep inside came strange feelings of pity, protectiveness and—yes, Artie realized—love. She hummed and swayed for a long time, then took the tiny, sleeping boy and laid him carefully next to their mother.

Chapter Ten

The following Monday, Artie went back to school. Except for Eula and Miss Small, no one had missed her. She decided not to let it hurt her feelings. Students often stayed home to help out, especially the older ones, though it seemed to Artie that she and Ballard were gone more than most.

Saturday found Artie down by the spring on Big Branch, dipping steaming clothes out of a big black pot simmering over a fire. She fished them out of the boiling water with a stick and plopped them into a nearby tub she'd filled with cold water from the spring.

"Of all ways to spend a Saturday, this is not it."

She whacked the water viciously and jumped back to miss the resulting splash.

Her hands ached from wringing water out of Dad's and Ballard's overalls. Maybe we should be like old Mrs. Hobbs, down to Caneyville, Artie thought. Wears her apron till it's black and greasy, and then turns it over until the other side is black too. *Then* she washes it.

Artie wrung out her school dress and hung it up. Laundry day was the only day she was glad each person had only two outfits, and one good suit of clothes. And now there were diapers and baby clothes to wash as well.

It's not as if I'm the only one working, she reminded herself in an attempt to escape from the mire of self-pity. Ballard is up in the field with that stubborn old mule of Grandpa's, trying to plow the tobacco ground. She frowned. Don't know why Dad wants to make a farmer out of him when Dad hates farming so much himself, she thought. Grabbing another shirt from the pile, she wet it and scrubbed it up and down on the washboard, then threw it in the simmering pot.

At least the baby wasn't crying all the time now. They fed him milk to fill him up after Mom nursed him. His cheeks had begun to round out again. Artie smiled as she pictured Simon John's little face when she had bathed him that morning, then dressed him in sweet-smelling clothes before taking him to her mother. His dark blue eyes had locked onto hers— so content, so full of trust, knowing nothing of the hardships of the world into which he had come, or even seeming to remember the pain of hunger he had so recently felt.

And Mom's smile had been stronger that morning too. Bright, like morning sunshine in a clear blue sky. Dad's face, on the other hand, had been black as a thundercloud. When Artie asked Mom why, Mom said, "He don't like my bein' sick, and if you ask me, I think he's havin' trouble sharin' my attention with a new person."

He wasn't the only one.

Usually, the only redeeming factor about laundry day was that Mom came out and talked with Artie while she boiled and scrubbed and rinsed. But of course Mom couldn't come out this soon after the birth. Artie sighed and looked at the pile of dirty sheets and clothes that still had to be boiled in the sudsy water. "Buck up," she told herself. "Where's all that determination God gave you?"

Her thoughts jumped to her heritage paper. It had to be turned in on Monday in order to qualify for the contest. She had finally finished, but wasn't sure it would be good enough to beat all the other students'.

She kicked the rinse tub. When she was grown up, she was going to have one of the new electric washing machines that washed by themselves and did the wringing to boot. But now that Dad was digging the well, she would be able to do laundry right by the house at least! This past week, Dad had followed Pappaw Woosley's directions—fifteen feet from the doorway and fifteen feet down—and had hit right on the spot where two underground streams crossed. Now all he had to do was line the hole with rock, make some kind of wall around it, and they'd have water right at their back door.

Thinking of the well made Artie wonder if she had any dowsing ability. Maybe Pappaw would teach her

the next time she visited. Folks always needed water—
it might be a way she could make some money.

This thought sustained Artie until she fished the
final item from the boiling pot and slopped it into
the rinse water. Twisting and squeezing the last long
sheet, she wrung out the excess water.

"There," she announced to the birds and bushes
and blue skies of May. "Laundry's done. Finally. And
no one better get anything dirty all week." She hung
the sheet and stood back. Clean laundry was draped
over every available branch and tree, looking like
pieces of sunset somehow fallen to earth. She dumped
the tubs of water onto the fire, made sure the coals
were out, and stowed the tubs under a big bush.

Stretching her thin arms heavenward, she sighed.
Hunger nagged, as it so often did. Outside of a few
leftover corn biscuits, there was little food in the
house. Again. And Mom had forbidden her to go ask
Grandma for any until next week.

"Yer dad don't like his folks knowin' how tight
things is around here."

Artie sighed again. Dad had gone hunting that
day. Maybe he would bring home a squirrel or some

other kind of meat. The thought made her mouth water. Ballard was probably hungry too. Maybe she'd go get the biscuits, along with the buttermilk from the morning's churning, and see how he was getting along.

He wasn't. She could see that the moment she stepped onto the upper field. A few straggling furrows drew a reddish brown line down one side of the stubble field. Her brother's tall, spare form wrestled with the old plow, laboring to make another thin stripe. She could hear him urging Pansy to "giddap," but it apparently made no impression on the gray mule—she stopped and started and stopped again with blatant disregard for her driver, and the plow bucked like a yearling calf every time the mule stepped forward.

"Bal, I brought you some biscuits!" Artie yelled.

"Whoa, mule," Ballard said, and Pansy stood like a post, only too glad to stop work. Looping the drive reins around one of the plow handles, Ballard left her to drowse in the sun and plodded over to where Artie stood.

"Good thing you come when you did, Artie. I was about ready to murder that stubborn rascal."

Artie grinned. Ballard would no more hurt an animal than he could fly. "Let's go over to the shade for a little bit," she said.

Artie sat, leaned against a fence post, and savored her biscuit. The salty crumbs tasted just right with the sour tang of buttermilk.

Ballard sighed and stretched out on his back. "Artie," he said, "plowin' is hard work."

"Yeah, I know. You ought to have seen me when I did the garden. Fact is, Bal, when I get grown, I'm not going to work."

Ballard snorted. "How you goin' to manage that?"

"Going to hire help, that's how." Artie stared into her cup. "I've done more than my share of work already, and I'm only twelve."

"Go on, Art." Ballard poked her in the ribs. "You're always talkin' like that." He grinned. "Remember the time you decided to go live at Grandma's so's you wouldn't have to work so hard?"

Artie grinned too. "Well, she did say that if I lived there two years, they'd give me a pony. How was I to know she was going to work me to death?"

"Yeah—it only took one day and night, and you hightailed it for home."

Artie poked him back. "Mom and Grandma cooked that scheme up so I'd quit pesterin' Mom about all the chores I was having to do."

"It worked, didn't it?"

Artie stretched and yawned. "I guess. I still don't like all the work, but I just quit complaining out loud." She studied her fingernails—clean now from doing the laundry. "I'm not going to get stuck here, working like a mule all my life. I'm going to go to high school, then to college in Louisville."

Ballard rolled over on his stomach and picked a stem of grass to chew. "Hard to believe anybody'd want to go to school any longer than they have to. 'Sides, how you goin' to pay for that? You know Dad won't give a dime towards it. He says third grade was good enough for him, and that makes it good enough for everyone else."

The biscuit turned dust-dry in Artie's mouth.

"You don't think he'd keep me from going if I paid my own way, do you?"

"Naw," Ballard drawled. "Iffen he don't have to pay for it, he'd most likely let you go, unless you make him mad over it. He's right proud of how smart you are, Art."

Artie breathed a little easier. "Well, like I said, I'm not going to work so hard when I'm grown up."

"You can't live without working. Who's goin' to buy your food and put a roof over your head while you're taking your leisure?"

"*I* will, of course. Teachers get paid cash money. Besides," she tried to explain, "it's not working I mind so much. It's the *kind* of work."

"Yeah," Ballard said. "Like me. Don't mind workin' all day on a car, but plowin' all day is powerful hard work."

They were silent for a few moments. Ballard cocked one black eyebrow at Artie and grinned again. "What about havin' kids and that kind of thing? Girls is supposed to get married."

Artie wrinkled her nose at him. "Maybe I will and maybe I won't."

Ballard snorted.

Artie grinned again too. "If I do get married sometime, it won't be because I can't support myself."

"If you don't need the support, why would you want to go raisin' kids, cookin' food, and keepin' house? Ain't that what you're tryin' to get away from?"

"Not really," Artie said, picturing Simon John's tiny face. It was hard to define, even to herself. She stretched out beside Ballard and propped her head on one elbow. "I don't mind kids. In fact, I like kids. But I'll tell you one thing—I want my marriage to be different."

"Different like how?"

Artie considered. "My husband and I will pull together, talk things over, share the hard parts of life. And if he gets mad, he won't go off hunting and leave me to muddle through, and I won't fade into another room when things get tense and leave the kids to—" She broke off.

Ballard nodded.

"Don't tell anybody, Art, but I'm plannin' to ask Walt at the Ford place if he needs a mechanic once school lets out. If Dad'll let me." A train whistled somewhere beyond Caney Creek—*wwhoooo, whoooo, whoo, whoooo-ooooo*—long and lamenting.

The two of them lay silent. The whistle blew again, fainter this time, like the horn of a giant ocean liner far off at sea. The green hills of Kentucky and the deep blue sky seemed so lovely that it almost hurt. Artie shook herself and crawled to her feet. "I'd best go see how Mom and the baby are doing. Don't want her to tire out."

Ballard stood too. "Yeah. Field ain't plowin' itself, neither. Guess I'll see you 'long about suppertime. Pray I'll get enough done to make Dad happy. Or at least to keep him from being mad."

Artie watched her brown-haired brother mosey back to where Pansy waited in the spot he'd left her.

"Giddap, ya ol' haybag," he said, and snapped the reins down.

Pansy turned her head as if to ask, "Did you say something?"

Chapter Eleven

Artie revised and rewrote her essay several times that weekend. On Sunday evening, she leaned back in her chair and read it over one more time.

> Heritage is more than land or money. Money can disappear. Land can be sold. But a heritage is forever.
>
> Our heritage began countless generations before we were born. Ancestors we may not even be aware of have passed on to us the priceless things of life—who they were, what they believed, what they lived for, and what they were willing to die for.

My ancestors have never had much of what might be called riches. They've never owned big horses or had a lot of land and livestock. But whether they were facing enemy gunfire in the Revolutionary War or guiding a flatboat down the Ohio River on their way to settle on the Kentucky frontier, they didn't look at their situations and despair. They kept going—on past comfort. On past tired. They had the determination to survive and that is why I am alive today.

After all the working and reworking she'd done, every word was as familiar to her as her own face. She skipped down and read the final paragraph to see if it sounded dramatic enough.

That is why I say that heritage is the sum total of those that came before us. But, it is even more. Like the last pearl in a still unfinished necklace, we are connected to our forefathers. In each of us is a little of them. Some of who we are, what we love, what we labor for, will be passed on to our children, our grandchildren, and our great-grandchildren. And someday, down the road, the strand of heritage will stretch beyond you or me and touch people as yet unborn.

The next day at school, Miss Small called for all the essays. Artie pulled hers from her book and turned it in. Sarah Jane took out her paper as well. Artie frowned as her seatmate handed her neatly written pages to the teacher. It didn't seem right, somehow, for someone who had no need of the money to make it harder for someone who did. Mr. Bratcher could pay for Sarah Jane's high school as easy as taking a breath, and college too, for that matter.

Back home that afternoon, Artie nuzzled her nose deep into Simon's tiny neck to smell the baby smell.

"How're you doing today, Mom?" she asked.

"Doin' good. Baby slept better today."

"Good, good," Artie said. She'd pretty much given up on finding Mason Embry's treasure, but maybe she would go dig roots if Mom didn't need her. So much had happened—Aunt Milly, May Meeting, Simon's birth—that she hadn't been able to dig anything since those first four pounds. Even if she won the prize and got money for school, the Depression was deepening and the family needed food. Anything she could contribute would help.

After changing out of her school dress into Ballard's old overalls, Artie was soon tramping along through the underbrush. How things had grown up since she'd last been in the woods! Chiggers would be out by now. She hated the tiny red bugs that climbed on and had a meal before they dropped off, leaving a welt that itched like fire and took weeks to fade. She thought of the summer she'd gone blackberry picking with her cousins, and they'd come home infested with the insects. Giggling, they'd lain on their backs on the parlor rug while Mom dug the chiggers out with her fingernail and daubed kerosene on the spots.

Beating her way through briars and vines, dragging a burlap gunnysack and her shovel behind her, Artie watched for the umbrella-like leaves of the mayapple plant. The soil was just right for digging, and in an hour or two, Artie had uncovered almost twenty pounds of the pencil-sized, pulpy roots. Too bad they shrink up so much, she thought. She still had to wash them and lay them out to dry until they broke when she bent them. Otherwise they'd mold and she'd have to throw out the whole lot. She'd probably only get five pounds of dried roots out of twenty fresh. Twenty-five cents.

Then again, there was always a chance she might find Mason Embry's money stash while she was digging roots. . . . Artie grinned.

Ballard was siting on the porch when Artie returned. She dropped her root sack on the porch. "Got nearly twenty pounds of mayapple roots, Bal."

"Good work, Art. Keep your eyes open for wild ginseng, too," Ballard said. "It brings a heap of money, 'specially the strange-shaped ones."

"What does it look like?"

"Don't know," Ballard answered. "Best ask Grandma. She'd know."

Artie visited Grandma on Tuesday afternoon. "Grandma, can you tell me what ginseng looks like?"

"Land sakes, Artie. Been a passel o' years since I seen any ginseng," Grandma said. "Best I can remember, it grows low on the ground and has three to five sets of leaves lyin' flat, like mayapples do, but made up of five leaflets each. If you can find some, be careful not to break the root. The Chinese pay awful good for ginseng."

Artie set her sights on ginseng, and the next afternoon she once more systematically ranged back and forth among the birdsongs and the verdant green of the oaks, hickories, pawpaws, and sycamore trees, dragging her gunnysack behind her.

But Artie found no ginseng. Either she just overlooked it, or the old-timers Dad talked about had already come and dug it out.

"Sometimes when people got too old to work, they'd go a-diggin' herbs to bring in a little cash money," he'd told her. "And they didn't keep to their own neck of the woods, neither."

Artie stabbed the dirt with her shovel. No treasure. No ginseng. She was inches away from giving up the root-gathering business altogether, but the thought of quitting filled her with more hopelessness than the prospect of twenty pounds of mayapple roots shrinking down to five.

By Thursday she estimated she had dug almost sixty pounds of roots. They were laid out on a sheet on one end of the porch, drying slowly. It would be at least another week before they would be dry enough to sell. All that work for about forty-five cents. Artie sighed. Nine cents toward high school.

Friday afternoon found her in the woods again. After working an hour or more, she plopped down to rest by an ancient oak. Sweat trickled down her back and made her armpits prickle. As she leaned back, a cool breeze flowed over her wet skin. Yet no wind stirred the trees. She looked around. Where was the air coming from? She turned until it blew straight into her face, and stared.

All she could see was brush and briars, rocks, and fallen trees. Then suddenly, like one of those illusion pictures Miss Small liked to show them where there was a picture within a picture, Artie realized she was staring directly at a big gap in a limestone outcropping. It was almost hidden behind the oak she leaned against.

Heart thumping against her ribs, she inched forward. The cool air blew from the lips of the hole, which was actually more like a big slit in the rock layer. Uncle Arnold said that air blowing from a hole indicated a big cavern farther in.

That's what it was—a cave! No one ever mentioned a cave in Grandpa's woods. This was exactly the type of place someone might hide his money. Maybe she'd keep it a secret and it would be her very own place. What a cool spot it would be to read her books in the heat of summer. Artie grinned, stuck her head into the hole, saw only leaves and dirt, then crawled on in.

Once inside, the damp ground sloped down and the tunnel widened. Her breath echoed in her ears as she inched her way forward on hands and knees into darkness more intense and solid than any she'd ever encountered on the blackest of nights. Somewhere ahead she could hear a faint and faroff roar, like water coming over the pour-off by the spring.

The dank air chilled her after the sunshine of the May afternoon. Behind her, the mouth of the cave beckoned her back to the safety of her known world. Ahead lay—she knew not what. What if the floor unexpectedly disappeared beneath her and she plunged into an icy black river that could sweep her away underground? At this thought Artie turned and scrambled back the way she'd come, bursting through the hole as if all her fears were chasing her.

There in the brightness, surrounded by warmth and the redbirds' cheery songs, Artie breathed shakily. What she'd escaped from, she didn't know, but one thing was certain—she needed a lantern if she was ever going to set foot inside that black hole again. Maybe she should see if Ballard wanted to come too.

No—not just yet. Maybe later.

For now, it was a delicious feeling to have a secret all her own. She thought of the basic caving rules:

1. Never explore a cave by yourself.
2. Always have more than one light source.
3. Always leave word with someone, telling where you went and when you'll be back.

But how was she to keep her secret cave secret if she had to have someone with her, and let someone know where she was? Might as well post a bulletin.

No. She wanted it to be her own cave, at least for now. Her very own—a place no one else knew about. The voice of reason whispered in her mind, "That's the problem—no one knows about this cave. How would they ever find you if you got stuck? Or injured? Or drowned?"

Artie shivered. She'd be fine. She'd go slow, not move any rocks or squeeze into any small spaces. She wouldn't go too far.

Memorizing landmarks so that she could find her way back, she sprinted home. She decided to take the old railroad lantern hanging by the door of the house. She toyed with the idea of bringing Dad's carbide miner's light along—the one he used when he hunted coons at night—in case something went wrong with the lantern. But touching Dad's hunting gear was a sure way to make him furious, and Artie decided she didn't want to risk that.

Little more than half an hour later, she once again stood at the black opening. She held the lantern at arm's length and crawled through the crack. With every inch, the passage grew wider and the ceiling rose higher. Soon the floor leveled out and the rock walls became a cavern as large as the Wilsons' kitchen. The roaring sound was louder than before.

Powdery red dirt formed the floor; dry leaves and sticks were strewn across it. Had the wind blown them down the passage or had some animal dragged them in? The idea of meeting a wild animal sent a shiver down her back, and she glanced around at the mouth of the cave, now a small slit of light.

With careful steps, Artie explored every foot of the cave, but found no treasure. At the far side of the little round room, the walls narrowed again and led off into darkness. Artie peered into the passage that led farther into the belly of the earth. It was high enough for her to walk in if she stooped just a bit. The floor sloped downward enough that she could soon stand upright once more. It appeared to be a long hallway, like a tunnel. Ten, twenty, thirty feet—the lantern cast spiky yellow points of brightness on the gray-brown of the rock around her.

There was an unearthly beauty about the cavern that made Artie breathe lightly and tiptoe as she went. If it hadn't been for the roaring somewhere ahead, she was surprised to realize, she would have felt quite comfortable.

Then the passage began to narrow. Before long she was bent in half, then crawling, as the walls closed in on her. The thin fabric of her overalls offered little protection from the stony ground, and her knees burned as she inched her way along.

Scooting the lantern ahead, she then crawled forward and scooted it ahead once more. As she crept along, the name Floyd Collins popped into her mind. Artie closed her eyes and swallowed hard. Floyd Collins was a caver from over in the Mammoth Cave area. *Was. Had been.*

Floyd Collins had been searching for a connecting passage from Sand Cave to Crystal Cave in hopes of bringing in some cash income. But while climbing out of a narrow passage, a boulder shifted just a few inches and pinned his foot. It took a whole day for someone to find him. He had broken all the caving safety rules—just like she was doing. Artie swallowed.

Rescuers tried everything from jacking the rock

up off Collins' foot to pulling Floyd out by a rope around his chest. But all efforts failed.

Artie shivered and drew back from the walls that pressed in upon her. Her lantern revealed no shifting boulders. Fresh air still brushed by her face. There must be another cavern farther on. With great effort, she forged ahead.

Just a few more feet, she told herself, and then I'll turn back.

The passage seemed to be widening. Getting up off her knees, Artie moved forward in a crouch. Then she gasped.

Before her was a cavern so huge and vaulted that the lantern's light couldn't reach the ceiling. Monster boulders studded the limestone floor, which had hundreds—thousands—of dimples, like captured ripples from some long-ago river. The roaring now filled her ears. On the back wall of the cave, water cascaded from a black slit, down to a pool of unknown depth, and disappeared to . . . where? Artie stayed far away from it.

All along the right side, rocks piled up like snowdrifts, until they spilled into the pool. On her left, three big rocks sat, almost like a throne. Artie eased herself onto them. A cold breeze blew on her neck, ruffling her hair. When she turned, she could see a narrow crack behind her, and feel a steady wind blowing from it. There must be a big cavern back there somewhere, but even if she could crawl into an opening so small, this was definitely far enough to go alone.

She swept the shadowy room with her eyes. Where would Grandpa Embry have hidden his cash? The floor was solid limestone, and she saw no signs of digging. There were no niches in the wall, and the crack behind her was too small for a man's hand to reach inside.

Artie slumped onto the rock throne, and as she did so, she spied something that set her heart pounding once more. A tin box.

Her fingers shook as she grasped it. Mason Embry's money box? She examined the untarnished blue paint. If it had belonged to her great-grandfather, surely the box would be rusted. Or did caves preserve things awfully well?

She shook it. Something bumped around inside,

but no coins clinked together. Could it be paper money? Artie tantalized herself a few moments longer before opening the lid.

A book nestled inside—red, with black on the spine. It said *Record* on the cover. With trembling fingers, Artie opened it. She held the lantern closer to read the writing on the front page, then stared in disbelief at the message there.

To our dear daughter, Sarah Jane Bratcher, on the occasion of her twelfth birthday, July 14, 1929.

Chapter Twelve

Artie gritted her teeth. It couldn't be. This cave was on Grandpa Wilson's land, not Bratcher property.

She flipped the pages until she found the first one filled with writing. She knew she shouldn't read someone else's diary, but it served that blasted Sarah Jane right—she shouldn't have been on Grandpa's property to begin with.

Artie read the first entry.

July 15, 1929. Dear Diary, This is going to be a book about my thoughts. No one really knows what I think, so I'm going to tell you. My birthday was wonderful. Papa gave me my own pony, and I love her so. Her name is Dixie.

I think this is quite appropriate, since we Bratchers are really from the Deep South—the land of Dixie.

Artie flipped a few pages further.

Sept. 6, 1929. Dear Diary, Papa just bought a new car and it's the bee's knees. Mama ordered a new outfit for both her and me so we don't get dusty while out riding. I asked for pink, but she said deep plum was better. Anyway, I guess Papa's investments on the stock market are doing well. He said prices just continue to rise. Mama thinks he should sell now while he's ahead, but Uncle Jack says values will just keep climbing.

Artie wasn't interested in the stock market. She had listened to Dad and Ballard discuss it one evening.

"I only have fifteen dollars to my name right now, son," her dad had said. "Just enough to buy groceries for the month. How'm I goin' to play the stock market?"

"But Dad," Ballard argued. "That's just it—investors buy stock with money they borrow from brokers. That way, people with hardly any cash can get stocks worth five or ten times what they could buy otherwise. People are makin' lots of money."

Dad snorted. "Yeah, those investors buy stocks with borrowed money, then turn around and sell 'em for a profit, but they never really own anything, exceptin' on paper. Give me somethin' I can hold in my hand."

"But as long as it makes money—" Ballard began.

Dad's chin jutted out. "And what happens if the price of yer shares drops afore you can sell, and you have to mortgage yer house or farm to pay for 'em? What then?" He had slammed out the door. . . .

Artie thumbed through the little book on her lap, looking for interesting entries. Most were Sarah Jane's braggings about this thing or that. Then Artie found the entry for October 29, 1929.

Dear Diary, There has been a panic at the stock market on Wall Street. We heard it on the radio. Stock prices are falling and people can't sell their shares fast enough. Mama started crying when she heard that, and Papa looked positively green. I hope he didn't lose any money.

November 7, 1929. Dear Diary, Papa and Uncle Jack have had a huge argument. Everybody is upset these days. I just try to stay in my room or in the barn with Dixie. I'm getting to be a pretty good rider. I can even do small jumps, though I think if I showed Mama, she would tell me to stop in case I get hurt. I think the exercise is making me a little thinner, too.

Artie skipped forward a few entries, to January 10, 1930.

Dear Diary, Mama has been teaching me how to cook. It's funny, but I didn't know that she even knew how. I thought we just always had a cook. I'm enjoying it. I can already make bread and cake. The part I like best is the taste testing. Cook only comes four days a week now. Mama does the other meals.

Artie was interested in spite of herself. The entry for April 4, 1930, said,

Dear Diary, I don't know what is wrong. Ever since last fall, Papa has been so quiet. He never talks to Uncle Jack anymore, and he and Mama always stop

talking when I come into the room. I know something is on their mind. Also, our cook and maid quit coming altogether. Mama said she had to let them go. I guess they had work at home or something. So now Mama and I are doing the cleaning as well as the cooking. I don't like it. It seems like all I do is dust and polish and wash. Mama said we might close off the upstairs so we don't have to clean it. Thank goodness we don't have to do our own laundry.

Another bright note—Papa has a new team of beautiful gray horses. Just wait till that Artie Wilson sees us out driving. I don't think her family even owns a mule.

Artie's lip curled, and she flipped a couple of more pages, to another entry in April. It was dimpled as if sprinkled with water, and the pencil lines blurred in spots.

Friday, April 11, 1930. Dear Diary, I can't believe what has happened. Now things begin to make sense. The stock market crash—why Uncle Jack and Papa never talk anymore—why Mama let the maid and cook go. I overheard Papa and Mama talking tonight after I went to bed. I came down for a drink of water and happened—well, I guess it was more on purpose than just happened, but anyway, I stopped outside their door.

Our money is gone. We may have to sell most of our land, maybe even our house. And the gray horses? What I didn't know is that Papa had to sell our new car, and the man was willing to give him the grays as part of the payment. I thought he had just taken the car in for repairs.

Artie thought back to the look she had seen on Sarah Jane's face that day in the woods when Artie had mentioned the team of horses. No wonder.

Why don't they ever tell me anything? After all, I'm almost thirteen now, nearly grown up, but they treat me like a little child. Should I pretend that I don't know? How come this has happened to me, to our family? How ironic. Just this morning I stood up in front of the school and told all about how our family was so rich and had so much. I didn't even know that we are practically penniless in our big house on the hill. I feel so foolish now.

It just isn't fair. And another thing that isn't fair—Artie Wilson's mama is going to have a baby. I want a baby brother or sister so bad, but Mama won't even consider it. How come Artie gets to have one?

April 14, 1930. Dear Diary, Today I told more about my ancestors. Of course I didn't mention we have money problems. I just told about all the stuff we used to have. No one seemed very interested, even when I told about the Bratchers of England. Probably just jealous. Then that beanpole Ballard Wilson told a story of how his great-grandpa had buried lots of money in the woods. Maybe there is hope! If I could only find that treasure, we wouldn't have to sell any land, and maybe we could have a maid again.

So I went out digging in the Wilson's woods this afternoon and was caught by Artie. She's always so hateful to me. I probably shouldn't have pushed her off the steps of the school last week. I will try to be nicer to her.

At the bottom of the page there was a small P.S.

I asked Mama about a baby again. She told me to quit pestering. When I grow up, I'm going to have six kids. Maybe more.

April 23, 1930. Dear Diary, I did try to ask Mama once about our money, but she got so upset, I stopped. And I've had this terrible thought. What if Papa doesn't have enough money to send me to high school and college? So far, the only thing I've gotten from digging for Mason Embry's money are sore muscles and dirty fingernails. I just have to win the state teachers essay contest.

So Sarah Jane had her worries about high school, too. Artie refused to feel sorry for her classmate.

April 30, 1930. Dear Diary, I have discovered a cave! My very own spot. Well, it is on Wilson land, but I won't hurt anything. I will come here as often as I can. Maybe I will even bring some food and furniture.

Artie snorted and turned to the last entry.

May 12, 1930. Dear Diary, Life just isn't fair. Why should Artie Wilson's family get a new baby boy and not us? (They named him Simon John, teacher said.) That makes four children in Artie's family, counting her married sister, who you have to count. But only one in mine—Me. And now Artie gets to carry around that little baby and smile and talk to it, dress and feed it, just like a doll, only real. I want a brother or sister so bad. I was crying over it after school today, and Mama came in.

I said, "Why? Why won't you have another baby?" I think she wouldn't have answered me, except that I was so upset. But anyway, she said, "Times are hard right now. Children are quite a responsibility, and it only makes sense to limit the number of children you have. Besides, your father and I have our own lives to live, and it would be so difficult to have another baby, after all these years. It's been so long that it would be very hard to adjust."

I said, "It wouldn't be hard for me. I'd do all the work. Please, Mama, please?" She was quiet for a while, and finally just sighed, and said, "Babies are very nice, aren't they?" It almost sounded like deep down, behind all her arguments, she wants one, too.

Also, I forgot to mention that Artie finished the fifth-level reader at the end of April and moved up to my desk. I don't like sharing. And she is always bumping me. But I wonder what she's really like. . . .

Artie closed the book slowly, placed it back in the tin, and shut the lid with careful fingers. Her mind whirled with all the new information. She returned the blue box to the place she'd found it. Somehow it looked lonely lying there.

With the reading of Sarah Jane's diary, the excitement of discovery had drained away. Still, Artie took the lantern and explored the cave inch by inch, but she found no money and no trace that anyone but Sarah Jane or she had ever set foot there. At last she crawled back up the passageway to the first room and into the late afternoon sun.

That evening at supper, she felt strangely detached from her life after her glimpse of Sarah Jane's. Although she'd borrowed a new book from Miss Small—*Little Women*—right then reading didn't interest her, and she said little, just listened to Dad tell about the shrewd trade he'd made that day. Afterward, he took out his fiddle and laughed as he played all their favorite songs, but his gaiety and the music did not work their usual magic for Artie.

She looked around the small room. Lamplight

cast a kind glow on the dingy walls pasted with catalog pages to keep drafts out. The dimness softened the floor of battered wood planking. A cool breeze seeped through the gap in the windowsill, and stars twinkled in the black fabric of the sky. The warped wooden door had a crack big enough for field mice to come and go under it at will—which they often did. She drew her feet up and wrapped her arms around her knees.

Two beds, hers and Ballard's, dominated two walls, and each family member had a wooden chair in its customary spot.

Ballard leaned back in his, reading another magazine on automobiles he'd borrowed from the garage in Caneyville. Mom rocked slowly in her small rocker, patching a wornout knee in a pair of Dad's woolen pants. Artie studied her mother's thin face, watching it light up with the special look that always crept over her features when she listened to the old tunes— "Shenendoah," "My Old Kentucky Home," and "Amazing Grace."

Simon snoozed on Artie's bed there in the living

room. His new eyelashes lay dark on cheeks the color of creamy rosebuds, his tiny face so peaceful.

How strange, Artie mused. This house was really only a small refuge from the weather, a spot to gather, a place to eat and sleep—one of countless many scattered through the Kentucky hills. Here was her family, their lives going a certain way, in their own little world. Just across the hollow, in other small shelters, lived other families who had their own private existences, too, ones that she knew nothing about.

Her thoughts darted back to Sarah Jane's diary. Even the Bratchers had a life people didn't know anything about. And so it went, on and on, across the whole nation—united under one flag, yet so diverse.

Chapter Thirteen

Reason Wilson put his fiddle back into its case. Loosening the hair on the bow, he tucked it alongside the instrument and latched the lid. Then he leaned back in his chair, stretched, and said, "Time to turn in, chilluns. You got a big day ahead of you tomorrow."

Tomorrow? Saturday. What was tomorrow besides laundry again? Artie opened her mouth to ask, but her dad continued, "Ballard, you and Artie gotta plant out the baccer sprouts."

Artie's mouth continued to hang open and her black brows pulled downward. She'd planned on reading her book tomorrow after doing the laundry. Now that was out. She knew from experience that it was nearly impossible to read and plant at the same time. Besides, planting tobacco was a backbreaking job.

Ballard's face fell. He dropped his magazine in his lap.

"Can it wait till Monday?" he asked. "I can stay home from school and help you then. I was plannin' on seein' the shipment of new Fords that's comin' into Caneyville on the morning train."

"Nope. Looked at those plants tonight on my way in from work, and they're gettin' leggy. Gotta get them in the ground or they'll be too big to transplant. Sun'll kill 'em." Their father pretended to be a wilting plant under a hot sun.

But only Mom smiled. Artie's eyes narrowed and she clamped her lips. As if a couple of days would make that much difference to those seedlings.

"Well, if you think so," Ballard said in a lifeless voice. "Guess I can always see another truck." Though she hurt for him, Artie could have kicked her brother for agreeing so easily.

"That's right, boy. Always another vehicle." Dad grinned.

Ballard stared at his feet. "You want to wake us up when you're ready to start?"

"Oh, I—I'm not goin' to be here," Dad said. He fiddled with his pocketknife, clicking it open and closed. "Told a feller I'd go look at a mule with him. Promised him I'd be there. You'n Artie know how to plant baccer. You'll do fine without me."

Artie's supper threatened to come back up her throat. A whole acre and more? By themselves? "But Dad," she burst out. "Ballard and me, we can't do it by ourselves. Besides, who'd do the laundry, then?" She knew better than to mention reading plans.

Her dad studied his fingernails. "Do the laundry some other time. I said you'll do fine. I'll get back as soon as I can."

Artie heard the iron enter his voice, but couldn't stop herself. "Are you sure you can't put the man off till Monday?"

Her father's eyebrows came down and his black-stubbled jaw jutted forward.

She braced herself, trying to keep her teeth from chattering. "Can we ask for help? See if some of the cousins could come?"

Mom gathered Simon from the bed and faded into the parlor bedroom. Please stay, Artie begged silently. Please reason with him. Don't disappear. Don't leave me and Ballard alone to deal with him.

She looked over at Ballard. He stared at the floor, arms folded across his chest, a trapped, defeated look on his face. He wasn't any help either.

"Dad, please. I'm sure Uncle Arnold would let the cousins help."

Her father crashed his fist down on the table. A glass of water tipped over. "*No!* Reason Wilson begs from nobody. If you so much as breathe a word about our needin' help, I'll tan your hide right smart." He stood up, knocking over his chair.

"And I ain't breakin' my word. I said I'd be there, and by rip, I'm goin' to." He fixed Artie with an ice blue stare. "Missy, I better not hear another word outta you. You and Ballard be out there in that field at sunup, and if you don't make good progress, I'm gonna to know the reason why."

He stalked out the door and slammed it so hard that the special willowware plate—the one that Mammaw had given Mom on her wedding day—fell off the shelf on the wall and hit the floor with a fatal shatter.

Artie felt as if the floor had dropped out from under her and left her hanging in space. Planting herself in front of Ballard, she demanded, "Why'd you give in so easy?"

He shrugged, but didn't look up or answer.

She stomped to her mother's doorway. "Mom?" she said.

"Come in." Mom's thin voice exasperated Artie. There she lay, curled up on the bed with her back to the world, as if it didn't exist.

Artie stood by the bed. Words fizzed up inside her chest, like root beer left too long in the bottle. Afraid of what she might say if she got started, she bit her lip and fingered the edge of the patchwork quilt.

Finally Mom rolled over and said, "Artie, try to understand your pap. It's not exactly like it looks." She laid her frail hand on Artie's. Artie pulled away.

"What else can it be? He's leavin' us to work while he goes and has fun."

"But he told that feller he'd be there, he didn't know the baccer'd be ready to plant out."

Artie snorted. "Well, if he cared about getting it in the ground, the least he could do is stay here and help us. I don't see what's wrong with him just telling the man that our tobacco wants planting. He could arrange to go see the mule as soon as the crop is in. Anybody else'd do that."

"But Artie, Dad ain't just anybody else. The way he looks at it, if he says he's goin' to do somethin', that means he's give his word."

Artie rolled her eyes.

"You know the Wilsons never had much money," Mom said. "I sometimes think Dad feels like his word of honor is the one thing of value that he has."

"What about his word of honor to his wife and family? Doesn't that count for something? Besides, it wouldn't be going back on his word to put the man off. He'd still go see the mule."

"Yeah, I know, Artie," Mom said. "But that's not the way yer father sees it. To him it would be breakin' his word. He said it. He's got to do it. It's too bad the baccer is ready now, but he'd let every seedlin' die rather than go back on his word."

Artie sniffed. "More like he'd let every seedling

die rather than risk someone thinking less of him or missing a chance to ramble. Mom, if his word of honor was important to him, he'd make sure his family had enough food and clothes. I'm hungry almost every day, but Dad doesn't see. He's too busy trying to look good and to have a good time."

For a long while, Mom was silent. At last she said, "Artie, when yer sister, Liddie, was just a little babe, your father was going to play fiddle at some dance. I asked him to stay home with me. He told me then and there that if me and any kid got in the way of what he wanted to do, he'd just up and leave." A tear trickled down her cheek.

"Maybe I should'a stood up to him then, but I love him, ya know, and I didn't have no place to go but back to Ma and Pa. It seemed so painful to think of him leaving me, of Liddie having no papa, of havin' no more children, that I gave up tryin' to face up to him."

Artie resisted the sympathy welling up inside. "We don't have a papa anyway," she blurted out. "He's not here for what we need—he's here for what he needs. And I don't care if it's bad of me to think that or not. I'm not going to disappear or ignore it and pretend like Dad is perfect." Artie wanted to add *like you do,* but instead she stood up and stomped to the door.

"Artie?" Mom said, her voice quiet.

Artie half turned. "What?"

"If you only see people's bad points, it blinds you to their good points. Try to see the good with Dad and let the bad go. He's a wonderful man in some ways."

Artie snorted. "And terrible in others."

"I know," Mom said. "But when I married, I promised God that I would stay with your father for richer, for poorer, the good with the bad, in sickness and health. I vowed afore witnesses that only death would separate me from him. I'm not sayin' it's been an easy promise to keep. But women have their honor, too."

When Mom said that, a little spark of understanding flickered in Artie's chest. She sighed. "I'm going outside for a bit."

The air had that after-the-sun stillness wrapped in velvety, star-spangled dark. Frogs were singing in the creeks, and bats swooped overhead. Artie rubbed her eyes and breathed deep the moist Kentucky air.

Mom was right about needing to see a person's good points as well as their bad points. But it was wrong to pretend Dad did no wrong just so he wouldn't get angry. Artie and Liddie had talked this over more than once, before Liddie married and left home.

Liddie had said, "There's a world of difference between choosing to love someone in spite of their failings, and letting them squash the life out of you."

Artie remembered Liddie's thin, brave face with its frame of dark, wavy hair as she said, "Just remember, Artie—you don't have to cover for someone else's wrongdoings. If you do, they may never change. Each person is responsible for his or her own choices."

This wasn't Artie's fault. She shouldn't have to fix Dad's problems, only her own. She took another deep breath, trying to rid her chest of tightness. Over by the barn, Ol' Friendly mooed. Artie wondered if the milk cow had run out of hay, and decided to check. Rounding the side of the house, she almost collided with her father.

"Oh, hi, Dad," she said. She was near enough to smell the familiar odors of sweat and soap and longed to bury her face in his chest, hear the rumbling of his voice against her ear like the purring of a cat, and to feel her tension melt away. For one brief second Artie thought he might pull her to him and hold her close.

But he sidestepped her without a word and went on his way.

Sleep was a long time in coming that night.

Chapter Fourteen

The next thing she knew, Ballard was shaking her awake. Though the sun was just painting the morning sky with a pale pink wash, Dad had already left. Artie rubbed sleep out of her eyes as she fried a couple of eggs for herself and Ballard, and before long they were carrying a washtub full of tobacco seedlings to the patch of field that Ballard and Pansy had plowed and made ready.

The late May sun gained heat quickly. Artie could already feel sweat, like dew over her skin, trickling down her back. With a hand spade, she dug a small hole in the earth, stuck a tired plant in, and snugged the soil around its roots. "One down, a million to go," she muttered.

Ballard planted like a machine. He just put his head down and went. Before long he was far ahead of Artie. She dug and tamped as fast as she could, trying to keep up with him, but she fell farther behind with every step.

The tobacco field seemed to stretch for miles beyond her. Creaking upright, she braced her aching back with one hand. Ballard was already at the far end of his row.

Dad wouldn't make it back in time to help. They could pretty much figure on that. Most likely he'd pull in about twilight and charm them all with the account of his adventure that day, as if there had been no unpleasantness the night before, as if these weren't his tobacco plants at all.

She plopped down on the red Kentucky soil. Her hands were cracked and dry, her throat already as parched as an old hog wallow in July. She stabbed the dirt with her spade and stuck out her bottom lip. "Maybe I'll just quit right now," she muttered.

The whine of gnats and the wrangling of birds

swallowed her words like the land swallowed all their efforts. Even if she and Ballard could finish by themselves, next spring they would have another planting, all the hard work to do over again, for the hope of a fall harvest that would put food on the table come winter. Never-ending, that's what it was—an endless, hopeless cycle. What was the use of continuing to try?

Yet even as she thought of giving up, determination was like a hunger inside her, driving, impelling. Artie stared up at the blue sky. She had to keep on. No matter what it took, she couldn't quit trying to make life better. Never mind how hard she had to work or who did or didn't understand. She took a long breath, smelling the rich earth, and let the truth of her thoughts sink deep.

Long minutes afterward, she placed her right hand over her heart without the slightest feeling of embarrassment. "Regardless of whether I make it to Louisville or just the next farm over, I will never give up, so help me God." The words rolled over her like a solemn river.

She could see it plainly now: Determination was

the one great constant in her life. Grandpa Embry's treasure or high school were not the most important ingredients in making her dreams come true. Neither was Louisville, as if location or occupation would work some special magic. If the Lord could help her keep her promise to never give up, she knew that somehow her life would be different, no matter where she lived.

Artie stood. Taking up her cast-off spade, she dug a hole, placed a seedling, and covered up the fragile roots. The little plant lay wilted in the hot sun, but she knew the sprout would grow and become a plant taller than her head. And the thought comforted her.

The sun's last long shadows had fallen across the field, and fireflies had begun to flash their cool greenish lights before Artie and Ballard finished. Ballard threw a lanky arm around her shoulders. "Well, Art, we done it. You're a ring-tailed wonder when it comes to plantin' baccer. I had to chase myself to keep ahead of you."

Artie grinned up at him. "Sure, Bal."

Looking back at the field, she saw no seedlings—only a dark patch of soil. But the plants were there. Artie found herself smiling as she plodded back to the barn with the spades and the empty washtub.

Chapter Fifteen

The following Monday after opening exercises, Miss Small called the students to attention. "I have received word about the essay contest," she said.

Artie tried to read the teacher's face.

"I'm sure that there were many wonderful papers received by the college," Miss Small continued, "and we must remember that only one person in our area could win the twenty-five-dollar savings bond. I know it was very difficult to choose the top essay."

Artie glanced over at Sarah Jane. The look of intensity on her face was now no mystery, and Artie was almost ashamed as she prayed, "Let it be me, let it be me."

After a dramatic pause, the teacher announced, "The winner is James Carver of Butler County."

So that was that. No savings bond for Artie Wilson. She waited for the expected pain, but none came. With strange gladness, she realized that twenty-five dollars would have made it easier, but it wouldn't have really changed anything.

Artie glanced over at her seatmate's bowed head, and an idea flashed through her mind. As the day progressed, the idea grew into a plan.

Friday evening of the same week, the whole family—including Grandpa and Grandma Wilson and Mom and Simon—jangled down Buck Creek Hill on their way to the graduation ceremony. Fireflies twinkled on grass and treetops and everywhere in between, like earthbound stars.

Ballard wore a constant grin that said, "No more school." He suddenly looked so grown-up in dark pants and a white shirt, with their dad's borrowed tie, that Artie's hand crept up and found his. It wouldn't be long before he went away and left her behind, as Liddie had.

Pressing those thoughts to the back of her mind,

Artie held Simon until Dad helped Mom from the wagon, and soon the family joined the rest of the community inside the cramped schoolhouse. The ceremony began.

Eventually the two graduates, Ballard and Marcus, came forward to accept their diplomas. Then Miss Small made a short speech, someone said a prayer, and the 1929–1930 school year at Buck Creek School, Kentucky, was over.

Artie made her way through the milling crowd to where her family was grouped, laughing and talking and shaking hands with friends and neighbors. "Mom," she said. "May I hold Simon for a while?"

"Sure." Her mother handed the baby to Artie.

Artie worked her way to the far side of the schoolroom. Sarah Jane must have seen her approaching, for the other girl's eyes grew wide. Artie could tell they were riveted on little Simon, cuddled so trustingly in her arms.

Artie had planned to ask if Sarah Jane wanted to hold him, but in the end she just placed him in her classmate's round, white arms without a word. The wonder and longing she saw in Sarah Jane's face was almost painful. Artie blinked away sudden tears and swallowed several times.

"Oh, Artie," Sarah Jane whispered. "He's just beautiful! Could I go show him to my mother?"

"Sure." Artie followed Sarah Jane to where the Bratchers stood near the door.

"Look, Mama. Look, Papa," Sarah Jane gushed. "It's Artie's new baby brother. Isn't he the most wonderful baby there ever was?"

Sarah Jane's mother reached out a work-reddened hand and stroked the baby's soft head, rearranging the snowy blanket around his little face. Artie saw the longing glance she gave Mr. Bratcher. He looked away.

Sarah Jane seemed to be in her own little world, a world that contained only herself and the baby in her arms. She drifted over to some chairs and sat staring at Simon, whispering to him and trying to get him to smile. Artie followed and perched on the chair beside her.

Long moments passed. Far away, out in the darkness of the early summer evening, came the whistle of the night train, like a fairy horn in the distance. At last Sarah Jane looked up.

"Artie," she said, "if you will visit me this summer, we can dress up in all the old clothes from the Civil War that I have in a trunk at my house."

Artie hardly knew how to reply. Finally she said, "I'd like that. And maybe you can come over to my house sometime and help me take care of Simon."

When she saw the effect of her words on Sarah Jane, Artie knew they were worth more than ten winning essays, or any savings bonds.